I0607988

I Wish You Were Mine
A Historical Novel of World War II

**A Story of
Love, Desire, and Expectation**

Marlene Joyce
Michael Charles

Copyright 2013 Marlene Joyce and Michael Charles

All rights reserved.

Art by Charles Fredrick

ISBN: 978-1-938886-12-6

www.iwishyouweremine.com

This book is dedicated to all who suffered, died, or otherwise became victims of World War II regardless of nationality.

We are indebted to our friend and his business
for assistance in research for this book:

Helmut Linden Lt. Col. (ret)
Philately
Postal Stationery & Thematic Material
Postbox 250206
D-50518 Cologne, Germany

Note from Authors

This story took place during World War II and afterward. It is based on true relationships and events. Certain historical figures, places, and events have been included to establish the period and historical times in which the two main characters lived. Their depiction is as accurate as possible based upon research of the Second World War era. The relationship of the main characters with historical figures, as well as their names, has been fictionalized.

Hitler's New Germany

Frieda anxiously rushed to meet her lover. As she hurried down the street, she noticed a small group of people had gathered on the corner where they had agreed to meet. He was a head above all others, not alone by height, but rather by his gentle, strong, and handsome presence. He was of Dutch descent; his was a serious face with pale skin, and he was currently deeply concerned with the matters at hand.

Some of Hitler's uniformed SD (the Security and Intelligence agency of the SS) and several plainclothes agents pressed the crowd away and back from the vicinity of the growing incident. The person of interest to the police and agents was Frieda's beloved Dirk — both lover and confidant. Frieda, shaken by what she was seeing, stopped abruptly and watched from the steps of a nearby building, remaining a silent part of the small gathering of onlookers. Her heart was controlled only by fear of the police and her knowledge of what might be the reason her love was being detained. She choked back the urge to shout and run to the rescue of the man she loved. However strong-willed she was, she struggled and held herself back knowing her consolation and, perhaps, retribution could only be found in remaining at liberty so she could find out why Dirk had been arrested and then work to regain his freedom. But her heart was sickened by what she saw, and she could barely keep from bursting into tears.

The uniformed police moved to arrest Dirk and physically force the young professor into the back of a long, black limousine driven by one of the plainclothes agents. As he was pushed and shoved by the police, he briefly looked around and caught Frieda's eye. A deep and unsettling feeling came over her, and she wondered if this could possibly prove to be her last contact with him. Both of them instinctively knew that his final destination might very well be Dachau, a concentration camp for people opposed to National Socialism. It was a camp from which, it was rumored, it might be difficult or impossible to get released.

For Frieda, the scene of the uniformed security police arresting her man would stick in her mind for many years to come. The image that would always come back to her was the flat tops of their military hats alongside Dirk with his dark, combed-back hair and black-rimmed glasses. She would remember only the tops of their hats, sparing her the pain of seeing the faces and identities of those who were, like jackals, roughly pushing and shoving at this man with whom she had developed a deeply emotional attachment and union.

The crowd that had gathered on Ludwigstrasse was seeing yet another professor arrested on a campus of one of Germany's institutions of higher learning. Their crimes had been simple. They had not gone along with the propaganda that was pouring forth from the government and National Socialist Party, nor had they encouraged their students to go along with it, either.

As the arrest of her lover was concluded and the back of the limousine disappeared around a corner, Frieda's life and destiny had been changed. But for her, standing on the building steps now, there was to be an immediate future filled with dangerous activity and the frightening reality of a Germany swept up and plunging toward a destiny as yet unknown to its trusting, patriotic, and eager population.

They had made a handsome couple. Frieda had the power to attract. She had straight, shoulder-length, dark brown hair curled up at the ends in a style that was popular on the continent and at home. It was brushed smooth and simple with classic grace and beauty. She wore lipstick, bringing brightness to her complexion. Wherever they had gone on campus, student eyes followed, but now all that seemed to have come to an end, an end that neither she or her love had anticipated.

Dirk's Arrest

It was mid-March 1939 and Dirk stood waiting at the corner of Ludwigstrasse and Schellingstrasse for Frieda. He had just left a class he had been teaching on the university campus and looked forward to an interlude with Frieda at a café down the street. She hadn't appeared yet, and he looked around to see if he could see from which way she would appear.

Two black Mercedes glided to the curb, close to the corner, and several uniformed members of the SD got out of one of the cars at the same time as several men in plainclothes got out of the other vehicle. They all approached Dirk, who was now aware that they were coming to speak to him—or worse. One of the plainclothes men flashed his Gestapo disc for Dirk to see and said, "Pardon me, Professor de Vries, but we would like to speak to you." Dirk stood his ground and the four men walked up to him and took up positions around him. The Gestapo agent went on, "We need to have you come to our headquarters to answer some questions about your teaching activities and associations. Would you please step over to the automobile and get in the back seat?"

Dirk didn't move, and as he looked around he noticed that his group was attracting some notice from others on the sidewalk and from people who were coming out of or going into nearby buildings.

"What is it you want? I am meeting a friend here, and she will have no idea of where I am if I just leave with you."

The agent snorted and said, "We'll leave someone here to make sure that your friend Frieda gets back to her apartment without any trouble. Now please step over to the vehicle and get in."

By now, several people who were students or acquainted with Professor de Vries had gathered in a small group nearby and were watching the encounter. With that, the two armed SD men began to push Dirk towards the parked vehicle, ignoring the small watching group.

Personal identification disc of a member of the Gestapo office in Dachau.

As Dirk was pushed toward the vehicle, he took one last glance around to see if he could see Frieda and noticed that she was standing on the steps of a nearby building, watching the proceedings. He averted his eyes quickly and got into the vehicle with the SD men. He noticed that one of the Gestapo men stayed behind as the two vehicles moved away from the curb and into traffic.

It didn't take long for the two vehicles to get to the corner of Brienner and Türkenstrasse where Gestapo headquarters was located. After parking the cars, the three men escorted Dirk into the building and up the stairs to an office door, outside of which was a desk with an armed SD man acting as a receptionist. One of the Gestapo men spoke briefly to the receptionist who picked up the telephone and made contact with someone within the office. Dirk and the two Gestapo agents were then admitted to the office where, after a short wait, they entered an adjoining office where a man in civilian clothes was seated behind a desk.

"Good afternoon, Professor de Vries. My name is Schreiber, and I have been assigned to take your statement and handle your case. Please be seated."

One of the Gestapo agents left the room as Dirk and the other agent took a seat in front of Schreiber's desk. Herr Schreiber then said, "We have had reports from students and some of the faculty at the university that you have made some questionable statements about your beliefs regarding National Socialism and where Germany is headed. You are a Dutch citizen, and there was a time when we would overlook opinions of foreigners in our country. But now, and since you have taken a position teaching philosophy to our young people at the university, we have to take another view of the matter."

He went on saying, "We are trying to build a new Germany here, Herr Professor, and, since you are Dutch, you doubtlessly do not appreciate the pain, suffering, and chaos that was Germany following the close of the last war. National Socialism is a result of that chaos and our battle with the communists and socialists who want to make our country a colony of the Soviet Union. We look very dimly on efforts by anyone who tries to counter the good that we have been doing here and the new proud Germany that has arisen from the humiliation forced on us mainly by Britain, France, and the United States.

"That is why you are here today. You have come into our country and evidently feel you know better than Germans what we should be thinking and the actions we should take to remake Germany into a strong nation, one that can resist communist and socialist upheavals and withstand the competition from neighboring countries who didn't think twice before humiliating us and causing people here to starve and to have to eat shoe leather."

Schreiber continued, "We have taken statements from a number of your colleagues at the university and from certain students. These individuals did not appreciate the tone of your comments and their negative influence on the minds of young people on whom we are counting to support our new Germany and what it will stand for. I have the statements here if you wish to go over them to verify whether or not what they have said is true."

Dirk was not surprised at Herr Schreiber's comments, as he had had some vigorous discussions with students and some of his colleagues. Some of these discussions were taken poorly, and he knew what they probably had to say in the statements. Nevertheless, he took the statements from Schreiber and paged through them, not to determine who made them, but to see what they contained and whether or not they were exaggerated. While most of them seemed to mirror what had been discussed, several of them were embellished by comments made by the individuals. The embellishments amounted as slams against him, questioning whether he was Jewish or a communist.

Dirk handed the statements back to Schreiber. "Herr Schreiber, I am Dutch, as you have pointed out, and your country has permitted me to come here and take the job at the university. I have tried to present to my students a worldview and some of the philosophies that have prevailed over the centuries here in Europe and elsewhere.

"In the course of this type of teaching, one necessarily finds points in all philosophies, especially if they may influence political and social life that one disagrees with. As you can see by the statements, not all students or my colleagues have been taken in by what you may consider as my subversive efforts. In my student days, I enjoyed discussing these things and there did not seem to be reasons not to discuss points of view that may have been construed to be critical of the Dutch government.

"Furthermore, the government did not seem to want to regulate or punish those who might be talking about them. I don't find it surprising that you are taking the position you seem to be taking. In view of the way the government here has been taking a very active role in promoting its aims and its attitude and activities toward the Jewish population, I have a hard time watching these things take place in a country long venerated for its leaders in music, religion, and philosophy.

"Unless you expel me as an unwanted foreign citizen, I intend to stay here and try and bring to young people a wholesome view of the world and what needs to be done to make it a peaceful place for all of us to live together.

"I am not a communist, and I have not investigated my past relatives enough to know whether or not any of them were or are Jewish. It doesn't matter to me what they are. However, I do not like the treatment of a segment of your population solely because they are Jewish and who the government now blames for causing much of the past chaos.

"These same people are now being blamed for having too much power and wealth. I find it sad that I have to stand here and defend myself against these accusations and the inference that I am a threat to the German government. I wholeheartedly reject any claim that I am against Germany and its place in the world.

"I am especially sad that the police and Gestapo find it necessary to waste their time interrogating someone who has been invited to teach at your university and present and discuss the various world philosophies and their effects upon culture. I find it unnecessary and disturbing that you and your government seem to take teaching and discussing philosophy as an effort to subvert National Socialism and the government."

Herr Schreiber listened to all of this with interest, occasionally glancing past the professor or at the Gestapo agent. When he spoke, as Dirk ended his statement, he said, "Well it's clear to us, who must protect our country and its citizens from the intrusion of others into our affairs, that there is a limit to what positions outsiders here can take, what they can do or say, and how they fit in to our new National Socialist culture.

"You see, Herr Professor, we have our points of view, too, and they're aimed at developing a National Socialist citizen who is willing, able, and philosophically ready to support the goals of the new Germany. Our Führer is our teacher and has given us the leadership we need to build a new Germany that is fully capable of defending itself and its culture. We must be able to rid the country of any corrupting influence, especially if it comes from foreigners, communists, Jews, and whoever else may wish to subvert our goals and culture.

"Unfortunately, you seem to think we still live in a time when any philosophy, no matter how ridiculous or destructive, can be permitted to be injected into young German minds. This not only diverts these minds from the path National Socialism has charted, but it may actually turn them against our Führer and his leadership. We can't afford to let that happen.

"You may think that the things you say and teach, mostly foreign to our country's ideals, are worthy of consideration by our citizens. But I'm here to tell you that they are not. Furthermore, we're taking steps to see that these kinds of intrusions are excised from society so that the country is not weakened again by communists, Jews, or the futile hemming and hawing of people who still support the Weimar version of so-called democratic government."

Schreiber went on, "You've been in our country for quite a few years now. It's plain to us that you wish to continue on the path you've been taking at the university. If we expel you, it will make a martyr of you, and we can't take the chance that the contacts you have will not be exploited by you or others in Holland.

"There are many in France and Great Britain who would like to weaken us as much as possible and change the courses of action our Führer wants us to take. It isn't going to happen. I'm going to remand you to what we call protective custody for the time being. This means that you'll be sent to our re-education program at Dachau until we decide what other course of action to take."

As Schreiber paused to catch his breath, Dirk jumped in and said, "You can't do this to me. I'm Dutch and demand that you call my embassy and allow me to talk to someone there. I can't believe that your government is now sweeping up foreigners whom you deem to be subversives and putting them into a so-called re-education program in a place like Dachau. Don't you think I'll be missed and inquiries made by my family and eventually my government?"

Schreiber leaned back in his chair and said, "We're ready to deal with those eventualities, if they come. We've already contacted the university and told them that you have resigned your position and are considering returning to Holland. As for your American girlfriend, she won't have any idea what might have happened when she hears of your resignation. She'll be upset, of course, but time heals wounds and she'll get over it. She is young and doesn't really belong here anyway.

"The United States is a corrupt country run pretty much by Jews. We don't need people from a place like that mingling with our young people and further diverting their attention away from what is good and wholesome in our society."

Schreiber turned to the Gestapo agent and said, "Heinz, please take the professor to his home and let him pack his belongings and collect a few things he may need at Dachau. He is not to speak to anyone, and his presence is to be as low-key as possible. The large bags can be picked up at his flat later. If anyone tries to speak to him, they're to be told he's trying to catch a train to Paris and can't take the time. There should be no uniformed personnel present so as to allay as much as possible any thoughts that he's being arrested."

Turning back to Dirk, he said, "Please don't think that it will be possible for you to escape while we're permitting you to get your things. We'll take all the precautions necessary to prevent that. That is all. Heil Hitler."

Always Look Over Your Shoulder

Unobserved at first, one of Hitler's plainclothes men followed Frieda from the street scene of the arrest. Shock and grief enveloped her mind, touching the core of her being as she managed to walk home. Somewhere along the way, a glance over her shoulder revealed the nondescript face and figure of a German man assigned to observe and report her moves. This was a very common practice. Lurking in the background, these sneaks slyly followed people suspected of anti-Nazi activities. Even neighbor to neighbor, residents, too, turned their heads just enough to spy on one another in order to report suspicious anti-Nazi or unpatriotic behavior. With chins tilted down, eyes moved right and left without visible head movement.

On this particular day, Frieda was followed as someone of suspect who could be linked to the arrested professor. She resisted the urge to run and try to outdistance her shadow. She knew that this might result in her being arrested, her rooms searched, and bringing additional serious trouble, something she couldn't afford to let happen.

Instead, she entered a small shop, sat down at a table, had tea, and watched as the plainclothes follower slowly passed by and loitered at the next corner. After a short while, she got up and proceeded to her home, towing the agent behind her. When she finally found the sanctuary of her room, a sudden wave of fatigue overwhelmed her and, without undressing, she collapsed onto her bed and fell asleep. For the time being, the events of the past several hours and the man who followed her were put out of her mind.

With the scene of her lover's arrest burned in her memory, Frieda became hotwired and moved to conquer. This became the driving force for tackling the mental and moral issues she and her lover had faced with even more energy and clarity. She began to live in the moment, her waking hours broken by bouts of fatigue. Relief and rest came with meditation and sleep, her way of dealing with the brokenness and shock that filled her mind and heart. She tried to balance her faculties as she faced each day.

At this particular time in her life, Frieda couldn't describe the process of finding balance. It was obscure, and she guarded it in silence. She sought a state of equilibrium that canceled opposing forces. Frieda was empowered. She was able to make decisions. In not being a victim, she developed mental and psychological states of emotional stability. However, the state of balance did not last long in the real world; opposing forces worked overtime.

～

When Frieda arrived in Munich at the central train station in January 1937, she had been greeted by her uncle. She had come from America to study at Munich University in the Schwabing district of the city. Munich, the capital of the German state of Bavaria, was called the birthplace of National Socialism. Hitler had moved there in 1913, and it was here that he began his effort to bring Germany the benefit of his thinking and leadership. His struggle and eventual success set the scene for the political climate in Germany during Frieda's stay in the late 1930s.

It had long been planned that until she got her feet on the ground, Frieda would live with her father's brother and his wife in the university district near the Königsplatz. From America, Frieda's parents were comforted knowing their daughter was safely anchored in Germany with someone they knew, trusted, and was part of their family. Americans, wrestling with their own economic problems, received little information, nor cared about what was happening politically in Germany. Had they

11

known, they wouldn't have been so naive and complacent.

Uncle Karl and Aunt Grace warmly welcomed Frieda to their home and excitedly plied her with questions about the United States, relatives, and their life and attitudes about Germany. Frieda settled in to their home and was given a spacious bedroom that she used as her place of sanctuary. She immediately felt warmth toward her uncle and aunt. In the days that followed, she became comfortable with her surroundings and their presence in her life.

Before Frieda became involved with her student responsibilities, her aunt and uncle discussed their desire to take her on a little holiday to see some of the Bavarian countryside since she had never been in Germany. The trip would be a weekend in Schliersee, a small lakeside resort town about 90 miles from Munich. The excursion would also include a visit with their daughter, Frieda's cousin, who lived there.

So, several weekends after she arrived, they made arrangements for the trip and headed for the central railway station. Traveling by train, they arrived in Schliersee just before lunch and were pleased to be greeted by their daughter Sophie. Sophie was a plain but attractive blonde woman, several years Frieda's senior. Sophie's husband was in the German Wehrmacht and was stationed near the Polish frontier.

From the station, they walked to a nearby small restaurant where they sat down for lunch and spent an hour dallying over their drinks, chatting, and allowing Frieda to get to know Sophie better. After lunch, they walked to her small home near Schliersee Lake, a small but beautiful body of water surrounded by the wooded and partially pastured slopes of the Alps foothills.

As they all walked to the flat, Frieda observed, "I'm so happy that we are finally getting to meet, Sophie. We have this great distance between us. Uncle Karl, Aunt Grace, and you are the reasons I decided to come to Munich to study. It's good to be with family, and being with you and getting to know all of you will be one of the highlights and benefits of my time here in Germany."

After their arrival at Sophie's home and after having settled in for a time, Sophie called out from the kitchen, "Come, tea is ready. I've baked a cake just for you."

Grace noted that her daughter had laid out her finest tea set for the occasion. Of course, all German households served tea or coffee in the afternoon. German women were schooled early to be fine homemakers and Sophie had taken to it with pride and proficiency. As children, German women learned to knit and crochet. Also as children, they cooked and learned to make schnitzel, preparing it in the same manner as their mothers, grandmothers, and great-grandmothers had done before them.

After tea, the family went for a walk around the village. Their stroll took them past a gastehaus and bakery, and they stopped briefly to admire and price the baked goods spread out in the showcase. Bread and hard rolls were wonderful and, if they had stayed overnight, would have been served for breakfast with a variety of cold meats and cheeses. Frieda noted that surely there was prosperity to be found in being a baker, cheese maker, and noodle maker in Germany. Sophie gave to them small jars of Erdbeer — orange marmalade — to carry back to Munich.

Sophie took them to a waiting horse and wagon that slowly made its way on a short excursion to a nearby village. This was a quiet and scenic ride through the fields in the countryside. People waved, showing their warmth and friendliness. A short visit to a gastehaus lobby in the nearby village revealed a formal portrait of King Joseph Ludwig I of Bavaria. His portraits were hung in many public places in Bavaria, but not as frequently as that of the new German leader, Adolph Hitler. After their return to Schliersee and Sophie's house, they rested for a few minutes and then started their walk to the village railroad depot.

As they walked, they said their goodbyes, and Uncle Karl and Aunt Grace encouraged Sophie to come to Munich for a visit sometime in the future.

Little did they know that Schliersee would become a quiet place away from Munich where the little children would be sent to live safely during wartime; away from the vicious bombing that would soon come. Many large cities, targets for Allied bombers, would send their children to small villages away from the bombing and the horror of war. Sometimes separated from one or both parents, the children spent their important formative years with strangers. In many cases, these childhood memories remained vivid into adulthood. Some were not such happy memories; the children, too, suffered trauma away from a united family.

Munich University

Munich University played a pioneering role in educating women — two received doctorates from the university in 1900. Munich was the second university in Germany to offer full admission to undergraduates, preceded by Baden. Adele Hartman was awarded a professorship in 1918, the first chair ever given to a woman in a German university.

Because of this, Munich became Frieda's choice for preparing for her doctorate. She appreciated its history of educational opportunity for women. What she was to discover was that anti-Semitism knew no bounds in administration of the university. Albert Einstein, renowned physicist, was prohibited from lecturing there in 1920, followed by other prohibitions of somewhat lesser prominence.

Frieda found that although Nazi ideology was intended to dominate teaching and research, only a small percent of lectures were overly Nazi in content. It was Jewish academics who were particularly targeted by the Nazis. They were firing them along with biology and political science professors. The Nazi attack on education nipped in the bud intellectual freedom and instruction, especially in fields where ideology of the Nazis could be challenged.

❧

Frieda was brought face to face with becoming a political activist on the campus of Munich University. Feeling the hole in her heart with the arrest of Dirk, fighting back became a necessity and dominated a substantial amount of her thoughts. She abandoned all caution in her quest for academic freedom for the Jewish teaching faculty; they were being carried off right and left by the German police. She was not alone. There were others engaged in writing pamphlets and giving lectures, demonstrating resistance, all the while hoping they could succeed in stopping the advance of National Socialism.

Frieda soon left the sheltered life that her uncle and aunt provided. She moved into a flat with middle-class friends whose parents were supporting them. They were intellectuals who attended plays and musical concerts. The group met in bars and restaurants, and sometimes in their flats.

The students didn't choose a lifestyle of self-indulgence but rather gathered forces in opposition to the Nazi regime. They spent hours discussing the philosophical, literary, and theological issues of the day. Before Frieda joined the group, they had engaged in a concrete plan to undermine the Nazi regime. This was not a political organization but rather a group of friends with shared interests.

Frieda gladly joined them and used a Remington portable typewriter, a gift from her uncle, to produce leaflets. Others copied them on duplicating machines. Mailings went to names and addresses in the telephone book. The message encouraged others to engage in non-violent resistance. A language expert would deduce that the author of the leaflets was a young romantic idealist rather than a leader in a dangerous resistance movement.

Recipients of the leaflets often turned them over to the Gestapo. Frieda's cohorts kept their silence with one another. Lives were in jeopardy. Again, the message was that Nazism was evil; make as many copies as you could and distribute them. So that authors of the leaflets would remain unknown, members each bought postage stamps from various sources.

Yet another author of leaflets suggested sabotage in ways that would disrupt the mechanical operation of the Nazi war machine. No real plan was put forth to undermine National Socialism in this way, indicating that the group supported non-violent resistance.

In an attempt to sway thinking, one leaflet mentioned the

guilt the German people burdened themselves with through the support of the Nazi war machine. The students were visionary in their ability to understand collective guilt. Since then, the German people have indeed experienced collective guilt, and it is alive after several generations. One German woman has said, "Why do they blame us?" She was born after the war, and to her it seemed unfair.

Gestapo surveillance was thorough. Frieda's group was under suspicion for being a larger group than they actually were with connections to other European nations who were not happy with what was transpiring in Germany.

Along Came a Spider

Frieda lived on the edge. Her senses were heightened. She frequently found it necessary to call upon an empowering energy; she found all that she needed at the time within that energy. The connection to the energy produced what might be considered miracles. The right people with helpful thoughts and actions appeared magically. Drawing energy from the universe, she found answers. She led the movement and, with her compatriots, carried off their campaign of resistance against the Nazi war machine.

Their group was growing larger. Frieda was placed in charge of finances, keeping careful records of income and expenses. They needed money to expand their leafleting efforts.

And one day, along came a spider. He appeared from nowhere and sat down beside her on a park bench. He was a small man with spidery limbs and the ability to spin a web of deception. Frieda was shrewd; she suspected that, although the encounter was a surprise to her, there was no doubt in her mind that the Spider had planned the meeting. He most likely knew exactly who she was and that she was much more than just an American student. The Spider introduced himself only as Hans.

"I'm a neighbor of your aunt and uncle. I noticed you when you arrived from America. I'm sorry that you left the comfort of their home and neighborhood."

Frieda commented, "I stayed in my aunt and uncle's care only a month or so until I could find a place near the university. It's strange that I hadn't met you or noticed you in the neighborhood."

Hans the Spider said, "I'm here to use the university library and happened to see you. When you sat down here it was an opportunity to introduce myself."

"It's taking some time to understand students and some of the issues in which they are giving attention," she said.

"If there is anything I can do for you, rest assured that I have many connections in Germany. This is my native country and my roots are here," Hans said. "If you should have any needs out of the ordinary, let your uncle know and he will contact me."

Hans and Frieda said goodbye, and he turned and walked away.

His name may be Hans, but he'll always be Spider to me, Frieda thought.

There were a number of political forces at work in Germany; there were the Nazis, communists, socialists, the Allies, nationalists, and a certain number of the general population involved in underground activities. Capitalists looking for a money-making opportunity were a silent, powerful force as well. Frieda wondered to which one the Spider might be connected.

~

Several times following Dirk's arrest, Frieda had gone to the headquarters of the Gestapo and made an attempt to find out what had happened to him. The first occasion seemed to set the pattern for the following visits. Frieda walked into the large building and went up to a reception desk set up near the building entrance. A uniformed and armed SS-Obersturmführer of the SD greeted her curtly with, "Good morning, Fraulein. What is your business here?"

Frieda responded, "I don't have an appointment with anyone, but I would like to inquire about a friend who may have been arrested several days ago near the university campus. He hasn't been seen since, and I am worried about him. Is there someone to whom I can speak who might be able to help me?"

"Fraulein, please take a seat over there, and I will see if someone is available. Who shall I say is making the inquiry?" the man asked.

Frieda gave her name, and as she sat down, the officer

busied himself on the telephone. After a short wait, he called her name. She walked to the desk and the officer nodded to an enlisted man standing nearby and said, "Please follow the Scharführer. He will take you to see someone who will deal with your questions."

Frieda followed the Scharführer upstairs and down a hall to another desk with an officer behind it. The Scharführer spoke to the officer who made a short call, and she was then led into the office of Sturmbannführer Heldmann.

"What can I do for you, Fraulein?"

Frieda was momentarily silent, gathering her thoughts. She then related her lover's name and the facts that led up to his being confronted on the street by the police and his subsequent departure from their rendezvous in custody of the SD.

Heldmann went to a filing cabinet and worked his way through a number of folders until he came up with what appeared to be one for Professor de Vries. "Ah yes, Professor de Vries has been taken into protective custody for the time being. He is being questioned about some of his activities at the university and answering some complaints that were received from students and others on the faculty. He should be detained for a little while longer, but I am sure that he will be back at the university shortly. He has talked about resigning and going back to the Netherlands, but for the time being he is being held. He is a Dutch citizen, you know."

Frieda wasn't surprised that there had been complaints about Dirk. She had taken several of his courses, and he had made a number of comments in his classes that could be construed as being hostile to the Nazi government. He was not one to withhold his opinions. His outlooks on the world and the philosophies he taught energized a freewheeling approach to his teaching and his comments at times.

He was not reticent about making various comparisons relating to the current mood in Germany and the flood of National Socialist doctrine that was being pushed in front of the populace.

"Would I be able to visit him and bring him some things to eat?" she asked.

"I'm very sorry, Fraulein, but that would be impossible. He

is safe at present and in no danger. No harm can come to him. I suggest that you go home, return to your classes, and not worry about him. He will be back with you before you know it. That is all I can tell you at this time. Scharführer, please escort Fraulein back downstairs and out of the building."

Following this, Frieda made two other visits to Gestapo headquarters but was unable to get any additional information other than what she had been told on her first visit. She became increasingly anxious and nervous, as it appeared that her worst fears might be coming to pass. She had a difficult time going to class and concentrating on her studies. At the same time, she became angry at the authorities for something she felt should not have happened and would not have happened in other European countries or in the United States.

Finally, several months had passed when she again made her way to Gestapo headquarters. Once again, she was in front of Sturmbannführer Heldmann. As soon as she stood before his desk, she blurted out Professor de Vries' name and said, "I think you know why I am here again, Herr Heldmann. I want to know what you have done with Professor de Vries. I have been here three times before and always you have told me to be patient and that he would be back at the university soon. I feel that you have been giving me the runaround. Professor de Vries is still in your custody and the least you could do is let me know what has happened so I don't waste any more of your time."

Heldmann sat impassively as she talked, and when she had finished, said, "Fraulein, you are a citizen of the United States. We have permitted you to come here to study and take back with you some of the wisdom you find here. Unfortunately for you, Germany is in the middle of a new era, one that you can't understand because you haven't lived through what we have. While we tolerate your presence and hope that you develop an understanding of what is happening, our patience for interference in our efforts to bring about a new Germany can wear thin.

"Professor de Vries has come to our country and has taken an active position opposing National Socialism. We cannot and will not tolerate that anymore. For the time being, the professor will remain in protective custody and will not be returning to his position at the university. He has resigned that position. I suggest that you go back to your classes and finish what you came here to study. There is no point for you to continue your inquiry with us. I don't want to have to take you into protective custody, too, or have you deported. This is the last time I will speak to you. Good day, Fraulein."

And, for the time being, so ended Frieda's efforts to locate Dirk.

Leaflet Writing

The group with which Frieda aligned herself was made up of intellectuals and writers. Frieda had prepared herself to author thought-provoking material, as they all had done. The model for the group was the historical figure, Mme. Germaine de Staël. She was a well-known political activist of her time and a woman Napoleon disliked and who had become a cause for his frustration. As a hostess, Mme. de Staël led discussion on philosophical issues as well as political issues of the day.

She published *Corinne* in 1807. At that time it was one of the greatest literary events of the day—as a work of art, as a poem, and as the romance of Corrine. The success of *Corrine* annoyed Napoleon. He was at war with half of the nations of Europe, not enough distraction, however, to keep him from following the activities of Mme. de Staël. Finally, Napoleon had enough of Mme. de Staël and exiled her from her native France. Historically, she remains known as a powerful influence of her era.

The sustained interest in Stael's thought and influence led to new paradigms for Stael studies in America in the 21st century. Mme. de Staël had become an international influence, especially for women. Since then, women internationally have recognized and honored her as a leader for liberation of their gender.

Frieda was following in the footsteps of her mother back in America who was a Quaker political activist and leader engaged in non-violent resistance. Like Mme. de Staël, Frieda's group attracted like-minded individuals, both men and women, to their salon.

Although written in a literary style, some of which were poetic, the leaflets Frieda's group produced contained information taken from laws that Hitler enacted earlier. The leaflets told of the human suffering and consequences of such laws.

The leaflets were a reminder that in 1933, the Nazis passed "The Enabling Act." The Act took away basic rights. This could be compared with the enactment of the United States Bill of Rights.

The leaflets addressed another concern such as the Nuremberg Laws of 1935, written to protect German blood and honor. Marriage of Germans and Jews was forbidden.

Reference was made of terrorism against Jewish businesses. In 1938, the "Night of Broken Glass" described the streets of towns and cities in Germany littered with broken glass from shop windows and businesses owned by the Jews. Nearly 1,000 synagogues were burned, 7,000 Jewish businesses and homes were looted, and 100 Jews were killed. About 30,000 Jews were arrested and sent to concentration camps. The Nazis forced the Jews to transfer businesses to Aryans, and finally, all Jewish pupils were expelled from public schools.

Certain books were banned. Visitors to homes might be suspected of noticing banned books and making a report. As an American, Frieda was horrified where freedom was compromised.

~⌒

Frieda looked forward to visiting with Uncle Karl and Aunt Grace. She needed more time with them to understand their position on the politics of the time. She was secretive about her own activities. Foremost in her thoughts was to discuss with Uncle Karl, his neighbor Hans. Hans was known to her as the Spider, the man she had met in the park who had mysteriously offered his help.

Both Uncle Karl and Aunt Grace had been German born. Frieda's father, Karl's brother, had gone to America where he had become a physician. The families had little contact over the years; Frieda was unsure of the political leanings of her uncle.

She was most certain that Aunt Grace was not a Nazi follower. Aunt Grace complained, "Hitler plans to conquer Germany with his screaming radio speeches." Fearing the buildup of a war, she also commented that for the big men, war is sport. Although the typical German woman showed little interest in politics, Aunt Grace freely made such comments in the privacy of her home.

Uncle Karl, too, was a physician. Her uncle was in the company of patients and colleagues daily. He learned to be careful with his choice of words and to be diplomatic. Talking with Frieda was different; he was not about to be partisan in any way. So they were all careful not to be put themselves out on a limb. Sometimes there were secrets between husband and wife. The secrets were meant to protect the spouse and spare them incrimination.

Aunt Grace served white asparagus for lunch. Boiled and served with a white sauce, the thick spears required more than a few minutes of cooking. Traditionally, throughout Germany, the stock would be used for soup the next day. White asparagus grew buried in rows of mounded soil, and when produced on a large scale, it required migrant workers to unearth the large stalks. It was hot, backbreaking labor. Frieda thought to herself that she much preferred the tender, green asparagus served at home in Philadelphia.

Frieda left after lunch, still uncertain about her uncle's politics. Before going out the door, however, she asked about Hans who claimed to be a neighbor.

Uncle Karl replied, "Yes, I've known Hans for several years. He has been a good and respectful neighbor. We don't talk over the backyard fence like some do; my time is taken up with my medical practice."

Uncle Karl failed to say that he and Hans occasionally played chess together. Frieda said her goodbyes to her aunt and uncle and returned to her flat.

Frieda's Lover

Tears burned behind her eyes but would not spill. She could not escape the suffering she felt for many months and years following the arrest of her lover.

Dirk de Vries was her love's name. They had met soon after she had arrived in Munich. He was a popular university professor with a significant following on campus. Frieda attended his open lectures several times a week; she was taken with his quick-witted presentation and personal power. A philosophy professor, Dirk cleverly punctuated his lectures with satire and his indifference to Nazi ideals.

He was Dutch, but he was educated in Germany where he remained to pursue his teaching career at Munich University. He was a fine musician, primarily playing the violin. Both sensitive and romantic, his following was largely younger female students. Many of his admirers had fallen in love with him. Since they had not met him personally, however, these emotions would better be described as a crush.

Dirk always knew where Frieda was in the large audience. It seemed she was sticking to the same general area, making it easier for him to keep an eye on her. Frieda was one of the older students and conducted herself with more dignity than perhaps did the younger students. Dirk was flattered and was most pleased when she repositioned her seating closer to the podium. Now they could establish eye contact. She walked behind the podium following a lecture one day, to compliment him on his delivery. They agreed to meet for coffee.

Theirs was a fast and intense courtship. For both Frieda and

Dirk it was good times and bad times. Falling in love without caution was a last effort to pretend that everything was right in the world. It was an attempt to clutch at a sense of order that seemed to be slipping away. The Nazi regime was closing in.

At the time, they did not have a name, such as mystics, to describe themselves. Both were endowed with a spiritual mystery, creating a consuming love and complete oneness with one another and the Divine. Their union lit up the universe as man and woman. They had a spiritual reality that was not apparent to their own intelligence or senses. Theirs was a most uncommon romance; there would be no such other in their lifetimes.

Later, they discovered a telepathic ability to have an interchange of ideas even though they were apart. In times of tribulation, these gifts were trusted as perhaps the only means of solace and communication.

Frieda was a musician; she had studied piano from the time of her childhood. In fact, when she began writing, she admitted that music gave rhythm and flow to her written compositions and various literary forms.

Dirk and Frieda had much in common. Not only were they spiritually blessed with a shared interest in music, but they were also struggling for academic freedom, for their own freedom, and perhaps for their lives as well.

Summertime came, offering a break from responsibilities for student and professor. Dirk and Frieda set off on a holiday. Although there was a sense of unease permeating the country, it was also a time to grab pleasure. Their courtship was a passionate relationship like neither had expected to find. There was no time to examine or define the bond between them. Nor could Frieda's mother, who was unaware of Dirk, offer cautionary advice.

The lovers experienced sexual vitality as the most powerful of all energy. Theirs was a mature love with a consuming and lasting presence. They basked in the warmth and satisfaction of their union, experiencing the lingering oneness of man, woman, and the Divine.

Dirk and Frieda traveled north to Cologne. The city was still a home for actors, writers, artists, and musicians. Frieda had prearranged the trip to coincide with a violin concert, a special treat for Dirk. Franz Keesler was on tour in Europe from America. Frieda was excited to hear an American musician in concert. Keesler had come from New York City, near her home in Philadelphia where her parents still lived. Keesler had studied and taught violin in Berlin earlier in his life. He was returning to the cities in Europe where people overwhelmingly admired classical music.

Americans tend to forget the Roman influence in Europe. Frieda found splendid examples of Roman and medieval architecture and with her active imagination, she envisioned Romans traveling the Rhine. She would long remember walking in the shadow of the Cologne Cathedral. Inside, the architectural and artistic details embellished with gold and precious jewels were spellbinding. The cathedral is the center of religious life of German Catholics and is the most important seat of an archbishop in Germany.

The history of the Cathedral of Cologne began during early Christianity. For centuries the building remained unfinished; it was not successfully completed for more than 632 years. The cathedral remains a beacon for all to see from afar. The spire was high and visible on the skyline, saving the cathedral from destruction. It was considered to be important for orienteering during the bombing raids that would soon come. The magnificent landmark would not be destroyed when it was vital for both the allies and the Germans.

Frieda was excited about a Rhine River cruise. They boarded in Cologne for the one-day round-trip cruise. Rüdesheim was the furthest point south from which they then turned and headed back to Cologne. It was a slow and relaxing day. The boat docked at several communities along the Rhine. Tourists went ashore, stretching their legs and taking a look at the vendors' merchandise. They had lunch in a dining room, and thrilled with panoramic views of the Rhine.

The trip to Cologne was the one and only vacation that Dirk and Frieda would have together. The dear, sweet memories became precious nostalgia. The vineyards along the Rhine, the castles that were part of the landscape, and the green space along the banks were a beautiful, timeless view. Frieda thought she could never find anyone in her lifetime that she would rather be with. She wanted Dirk to be her one and only lifetime companion.

～⌒◯

Missing her mother, Frieda dispelled loneliness by spending time with Aunt Grace. Aunt Grace lived within the shadow of Uncle Karl all the years of their marriage. It seemed to be a typical German marriage. Uncle Karl provided for her, and she looked after him, making his life at home organized, comfortable, and complete. Uncle Karl was the decision maker.

This did not mean, however, that Aunt Grace lacked knowledge about what was going on around her. She was well informed and had her own opinions, many of which she did not always share with her husband.

Frieda cherished the time alone with her aunt to discuss her neighbor, Hans. While they were having tea one afternoon, Frieda said, "Hans introduced himself to me recently while I was on campus. Can you tell me something about him? "

"My dear, your uncle and I have known Hans for several years. He has always been a good neighbor, pretty much keeping to himself. I do know that he and your Uncle Karl play chess from time to time."

"That's strange," Frieda commented. "Uncle Karl never mentioned that to me."

Aunt Grace said, "Well, I make myself scarce when the men play chess."

Frieda replied, "You mean that you never overhear what they talk about?"

Aunt Grace would not admit that she sometimes eavesdropped.

"Hans offered his help in any way that I may need. He said that he was German-born and had many contacts," Frieda said. "What do you think he had in mind?"

"Frieda, since you are an American, Hans may be digging for dirt about your political activities. I have no idea about such things where you are concerned, but I'll tell you one thing right now, I would trust Hans with my life."

Frieda had found the answer she needed. She said goodbye

to Aunt Grace, gave her a hug, and mentioned that she would see her again soon.

~⸰⁀⸰

After having been gone several days, Frieda walked through the door of her flat to find things slightly out of place. A box of candy had been touched. The dust on the table showed finger-prints that could not possibly be overlooked. An unknown per-son had illicitly entered her space, someone who had enough nerve to eat her chocolates.

She went to the bedroom to find that her bed had been slept in. Frieda was meticulous about orderliness; it was not she who had left the bed unmade. Her eyes moved to the bookcase. Books had been rearranged.

The intruder was self-confident, unafraid of any retribution on Frieda's part. He boldly violated her space knowing that he now held the upper hand with the evidence that he had found.

The landlady confessed that an unknown man had been in Frieda's flat. He entered under pretext of being a friend. When the man was ready to leave the premises, he told the landlady that Frieda held banned books in her collection. He threatened to go to the police and make a report. The landlady did not want to be implicated by having such a tenant. She managed to stop the man by saying that Frieda was an American. It would seem that Americans did not fully understand the restrictions that were in force.

For the time being, Frieda felt relief. Although relief took precedence, it did not consume her enough to overcome the revulsion she felt knowing that someone had slept in her bed. The stranger had rifled her belongings and eaten her candy. Sickened, she disposed of the box and remaining candy, stripped the bed of linens for the laundry, and dusted away the finger-prints on the table. The invasion of privacy was not unusual under Nazism.

~⸰⁀⸰

Frieda's friends no longer met as a large group. If one was under suspect, others could very well be incriminated. It seems that birds of a feather really do fly together. Frieda and her friends secretly continued their work producing and distributing leaflets. Individuals did not know details of what others were writing. In many cases, even the distribution details were hidden from one another. The group continued to need money to expand the program.

As the designated fundraiser, Frieda worked hard on the project. As bookkeeper, she kept records of expenditures and income. Money was secretly funneled from parents and relatives to the students. Donors did not always know how the money was spent; they were careful not to ask. As far as they were concerned, the gifts were made only to a student on campus who needed extra money. After all, they were doing no more than gifting to their family.

Hans the Spider had opened a door for Frieda that day in the park. Since Frieda had talked with Aunt Grace about Hans, she felt relief. Perhaps Hans' intentions were meant to be helpful without underhandedness aimed at her. Perhaps they were both on the same side of political action. Frieda rationalized that Aunt Grace most certainly would not expose her niece to the Nazis. Frieda made a decision to trust the Spider.

Frieda went over in her mind other known political action groups with which Hans might be affiliated. These political parties, too, were interested in undermining the Nazis. It made little difference whether it was Frieda and her friends or another organization working against the Nazis. They were all looking for the same outcome: undermine the Nazi war machine.

~⌒

In another visit with Aunt Grace, Frieda said, "I think that I'm ready to take Hans up on his offer for help. I'll be discussing that with him as soon as we can meet. Right now, I can't tell you what is in the works. Aunt Grace, you know my family background. I am an American, my mother is a Quaker, and my father is a physician. I can assure you that given this family legacy, my work and my intentions are on the side of freedom and justice for the people."

"Frieda, I'll let Hans know that you're ready to meet with him." Aunt Grace continued to say, "Go ahead with your work, my dear. Look for him in the same place near the library at two o'clock tomorrow afternoon.

～

That evening, Frieda wrote a letter to her parents in Philadelphia. Given the magnitude of the life and death situations in which she lived, Frieda felt best that she should write her parents and let them know. Everything was moving quickly; Frieda had little opportunity to sit and write letters; however, she was right down to the line for her own safety.

Dear Mother and Father,

Don't take on my pain; just give me comfort, I ask of you. It is time to tell you that I have recently lost the man in my life who meant everything to me. We deeply love one another and would hope to spend our lives together. His name is Dirk de Vries, a young Dutch-born professor at Munich University. Our courtship was swift. This is the way of many new relationships for people living in Germany today. There is a sense of urgency for us to live in the moment; we do not know what is in our future even tomorrow.

I was rushing to meet Dirk near the university one day. Standing on the steps of a nearby building, I saw uniformed police gathered around him. The police almost knocked his glasses off. The police arrested him, forcing him into a vehicle. It seems that more than one professor has recently run up against the police.

I have been in touch with Uncle Karl and Aunt Grace and go there from time to time; sometimes for tea, sometimes for a meal. I love them dearly; they help ease my loneliness and fill the emptiness in my heart when I am away from both of you.

Philadelphia certainly will look good to me when I am able to return.

My love to both of you.

Your loving daughter,
Frieda

Fearing censorship, Frieda had not given detailed information that might lead to discovery of what she was really doing.

Frieda awoke the next morning with trepidation for what she knew was ahead of her that day. There were some things in life that she simply did not want to do. Feeling frightened and depressed, she reluctantly prepared for her day. After lunch, she left for her meeting with the Spider. She arrived a half hour early, planning to observe from a distance any activity that might announce the Spider. Were there agents, perhaps secret police, who would detain her? She did not want to be a victim, nor did she intend to walk into a trap. Her meeting with the Spider might not be reported immediately. Surveillance could possibly result in a record of her activity over a period of time.

She kept on her feet, walking within eyesight of the bench where she was to meet the Spider. She felt less vulnerable being on the move. Fleeing the area would be quicker, with less detection of facial features, clothing, hairstyle, and profile. She carried a multi-colored handbag that flipped to the other side, showing itself a different color. The bag easily unfolded to become a satchel. Frieda wanted to be a chameleon, moving anonymously in the streets. A babushka would easily camouflage her hair. The sweater she wore, when removed, might be hidden in the satchel. Frieda was uncertain about her image and the identity all of this created. Was she a bag lady, an eccentric student searching for a unique identity, or was she a German hausfrau with a flair that broke tradition?

There was no sign of anyone who might be watching her. There was no sign of Hans himself. He was more experienced than she in such matters and was probably standing off somewhere observing her. Frieda moved closer to the park bench at two o'clock. Given German punctuality, she knew Hans would soon be there. Within minutes Hans came walking toward her.

"Please sit down, Hans. This is not a meeting of chance. It's good to see you. You mentioned earlier that you might be able to provide help when I needed it," Frieda said.

Hans commented, "I knew it was just a matter of time until I heard from you. My sources have indicated that you and your friends need money to carry out your program."

Frieda could not help but wonder if one of those sources

might be her Aunt Grace. They had not discussed Frieda's project; however, Aunt Grace may have guessed that whatever Frieda was up to would cost more money.

"We want to help you with your program," said Hans. "All efforts such as yours and your friends' are important. They should not be given a short stick because of the lack of money. I have an envelope for you with enough to help extend your program."

Frieda queried, "Are you with the Allies?"

"In this business, we make no declarations concerning our political ties. Fraulein, it is better not to ask these questions."

Hans slipped her an envelope, which she discreetly hid under her sweater. They parted ways, each going in a different direction. Frieda wore her babushka just in case.

More Fuel for Leaflets

One of the most heinous of crimes was Hitler's state-organized euthanasia program. It had secretly been established in August 1939. The Nazis were systematically killing thousands of mentally ill and physically handicapped adults and children in German mental hospitals. The killing took place using lethal injections, gas vans, and shower rooms converted to gas chambers. A German Catholic bishop brought this to light. He denounced Hitler and the euthanasia program. Eventually, the Nazis stopped the program of killing mentally and physically handicapped adults. The killing of children under this program continued in secrecy and was moved from hospitals into extermination camps.

The bishop's condemnation of Hitler and the euthanasia program was reproduced in leaflet form. Again, the leaflets were copied and distributed, fueling the non-violent opposition groups whose purpose it was to influence opinion.

∽

There was no doubt in Frieda's mind that she was empowered through writing. She was fighting for justice for her lost lover. Frieda's desire to write began as a child. She followed that path with her education all the way to Munich University where she had hoped to receive a Ph.D. in literature. Turmoil in Nazi Germany presented serious distractions from education. The union of Germany with Austria and the Czechoslovakia turmoil created a lot of troubling political interference at the school. Now the invasion of Poland and the beginning of a shooting war brought even more turmoil both on and off campus. Professors were arrested; students gave too much time to political action. Precedence was given to surviving the chaos. Frieda was rightfully concerned for her academic future.

Frieda could have just walked. She could have walked away and gone home to Philadelphia. What was her future in Germany? Dirk had been taken away; she did not know where he was or if he was still alive. She had communicated with him — reading one another's thoughts, so to speak — for several weeks following his arrest. Now, he was silent. There was nothing. She was losing hope.

Although it looked as though the Nazis were gaining strength, Frieda was unwilling to let them be winners without giving a good fight herself. The Nazis had caused her personal pain when they took Dirk away. Common sense overrode anger, reminding her that there was no way to change what had already taken place. However, she could continue to take subversive action through non-violent resistance.

Frieda and her friends beefed up the leafleting, extending coverage to several nearby communities. Again, they came to Frieda for more money. It had been a month since she had met with Spider. It was time to strike again.

She arranged a time with Aunt Grace to meet her in a local pastry shop. Oh, the cakes! The cakes were a distraction from what she had so seriously planned to say to Aunt Grace. They sat at a small patio table to talk and enjoy their cake and coffee.

"Aunt Grace, it's time for me to meet Hans again. Our first meeting went well, and I believe he's willing to help us further."

"Frieda, I can arrange another meeting with Hans. You should know that repeated meetings increase the danger to both of you," cautioned Aunt Grace.

Frieda said, "It's a risk that I'm willing to take. I've already gone beyond what once seemed normal to me. I've been placed here at this point in time, away from my parents and America. There is no precedent for my actions. There is no longer a sense of order or a sense of reason. I'm already out on a limb, so to speak."

"If you're sure that this is what you want, I'll arrange a

meeting with Hans," said Aunt Grace. "Make it the same time and same place tomorrow afternoon."

"Aunt Grace, thank you for your help. Tell Hans that I'll have a new disguise tomorrow." Frieda gave her a hug before leaving.

Frieda prepared herself for the meeting with the Spider. If this were not such a serious situation, she might have enjoyed her new disguise. She wore a blonde, pageboy, shoulder-length wig, making her appear stylish and dramatic in a tan trench coat with epaulets. Her handbag was brown leather with a shoulder strap. Her appearance had entirely changed; neither Aunt Grace nor her own mother would have recognized her at first sight. This was especially true since Frieda wore dress shoes with high heels, which was completely out of character for her.

⁓

At home in her flat, a young messenger delivered a sealed envelope. He had appeared on his bicycle wearing the official hat and uniform of a delivery service. Frieda opened the envelope with trembling hands. Who would seek her out to receive a letter? The letter was from Josef, a friend of Dirk de Vries. Earlier, Dirk had mentioned his friend Josef and their affinity with political issues. Josef was the quiet one, choosing a backseat position. Josef was afraid for Dirk who displayed open defiance of Nazism.

Josef's brief note said that he was enclosing a letter from Dirk. Josef knew that the information was meant for both him and Frieda. The letter, postmarked Dachau, had been directed to Josef in order to protect Frieda.

> *This is the only letter that I am writing. I was arrested, put in protective custody, and taken to the Dachau Camp where I am awaiting a trial. Until that time, I am working in a factory outside of the compound. My best wishes to you and all my friends. Dirk.*

Shaken, Frieda read Dirk's letter over and over again. At least he was still alive.

Frieda immediately wrote Josef a note asking for a meeting

with him. Soon after, he appeared at her door and introduced himself. Frieda invited him in and they had a long conversation over coffee. They exchanged information about what could have possibly happened to Dirk. Both were happy to know that for now Dirk was alive. They discussed what they knew or had overheard about concentration camps and how prisoners were handled. Dirk's letter was proof that some mail was leaving the camps.

Much later, Frieda would learn that the camps Dachau and Sachsenhausen were for protective custody prisoners with good records who were capable of improvement. Interestingly, in 1941, Dachau was in part intended for prisoners who stood particularly in need of consideration. Older people, political prisoners, and members of the clergy were employed in the medicinal herb garden. On the other hand, Dachau was known to exterminate prisoners who were considered to be enemies of the State. In some cases, prisoners were not given a trial in the special courts but were executed outright.

The Law of 1939 changed the criminal procedure, giving legal authorities the means of extraordinary intervention against verdicts regarded too mild. Consequently, the death penalty was used more frequently.

The day Britain and France entered the war—September 3, 1939, upon orders by Hitler and Himmler—a circular was issued, indicating that principles of the internal protection of the state during war required action. Any person voicing doubt about the victory of the German people or the just cause of the war, was to be arrested. This included those whose actions were particularly dangerous and far-reaching in their propaganda effect. The directive continued to read that these persons must be liquidated by execution.

Had Frieda known this information and details about the camp administration, she would have realized that Dirk's profile made it virtually impossible for him to be released from the Dachau Konzentrationslager anytime before at least the end of the war.

Bitte sorgfältig aufbe.....ren! — Der Absender
wird gebeten, nur den um....ndeten Teil auszufüllen!

Einlieferungsschein

Gegen=
stand: ....*) Brief.............*) Nr...

Nach=nahme:	*RM*	*Rpf*	Ge=wicht:	kg	g

Wert oder Betrag:				*RM*	*Rpf*

Emp=
fänger:

Bestim=
mungs=
ort:

Postannahme

C 62   Din A 7
(6 c 60)
StdW (4. 40)

Mail moved into and out of Dachau Concentration Camp. This form shows the receipt of a registered or valued letter sent to someone held in Block 3K of the camp. Block 3K was where priests and ministers, etc., were incarcerated. The item was mailed from Vienna in 1938 after Austria was incorporated into the Third Reich.

Protective Custody at Dachau

Dirk had endured what seemed like endless interrogation at Gestapo headquarters. His status as a Dutch citizen probably saved him from some of the more primitive methods of torture employed by the Gestapo and the SD. The interrogation seemed to focus on whether or not he might be linked with other individuals or groups, either within or outside of Germany, who could prove to be a danger to the Nazi government or the Führer. Dirk did not name others who he knew for fear that they might be linked to some fantastic plot imagined by his interrogators.

However, it didn't matter whether or not he named them. The Gestapo thoroughly investigated those who were associated with him at the university and eventually got around to his friends. After several months of on and off investigating, the Gestapo concluded that Dirk was not currently linked with any subversive groups they could identify. While they couldn't be absolutely certain, investigators were willing to agree that he was probably speaking at the university on his own initiative. They then brought the interrogation to an end.

On a cold, cloudy day in January 1940, Dirk was escorted from his cell at headquarters and brought before one of his interrogators, Dieter Manlo. Manlo had never appeared to be a member of the SD, and Dirk viewed him as one of the supervising Gestapo agents. "Sit down, de Vries. We are at the end of interrogating you, and I want to discuss with you what happens next. As you are aware, we have broken your affiliation with the university. We are going to extend your protective custody indefinitely.

Our investigation shows that you and your courses have been popular at the university and that you have had an impact on the students and certain members of the university faculty. In other words, you have built up a following among those currently there and those who have left the university over the years during the time you have taught there. We are not going to turn you loose in our society again, as some of what you have taught and said appears to be out and out subversive. We are going to hold you for trial in People's Court and let them decide what to do with you. You will be transferred to Dachau and the camp there pending your trial at some later date."

Dirk responded, "Herr Manlo, I am a Dutch citizen and ask that you contact the Dutch Embassy as I am under their protection. I have relatives in the Netherlands who will wonder what has become of me and begin making inquiries. Will you let me talk to someone at the embassy?"

Manlo's eyes narrowed as he looked at Dirk and said, "Herr Professor, we will take care of the contacts with your embassy for you. You may not talk to anyone at the embassy. This country is now at war and Great Britain and France seem to want to confront the Führer over our response to the continual attacks from Poland across our frontier with them. It appears the war will shortly be expanded. You may be much safer in Germany than in your home country."

Dirk was not surprised at what Manlo said. After several months of confinement and interrogation, and hearing from other prisoners what they were going through, he was now, more than ever, acutely aware of the extent of the police state that was being created by Hitler and the National Socialist party. The security people were leaving no stone unturned to stamp out any vestige of opposition among German citizens. The government was demanding strict obedience to the edicts it was issuing. The invasion of Poland and the declaration of war by Britain and France in September 1939 had put the Nazis on a war footing. The gloves were off and the military, SS, SD, and police reigned supreme in the country and could not afford to have internal enemies while German armies and men were facing external ones.

The next morning, Dirk was led to a waiting police van

along with several other prisoners, one of whom had been obviously beaten. They were handcuffed and helped into the back of the van where they were seated. Several armed SS guards sat with them. They were not permitted to speak to one another and rode in silence the 25 miles to the Dachau Concentration Camp just east of the town of the same name.

As the van drove through the gate, Dirk was heartsick. He had heard rumors about Dachau, and they had not been good ones. Now he was going to find out personally whether the rumors were true or just rumors. He thought of Frieda and how they had come together so effortlessly as a couple and lovers. He halfway wished he had listened to some of his friends who had advised him to not be so open about his anti-Nazi feelings. But it was too late for that now, and he knew in his heart that someone had to take a stand against what was happening. His conscience was clear in that respect.

The prisoners were unloaded in front of a nondescript, wooden, barracks-like building, and they were led inside by the SS guards. The building served as a reception center. A prisoner who appeared to be in charge of the clothing distribution gave each man two sets of a loose-fitting, blue-striped uniform along with a skull cap, underwear, thin jacket, socks, work shoes, and a belt. An SS doctor examined each of them and documented the findings.

They were then led to a desk where they were interrogated for several minutes, tattooed with their prisoner number, and finally handed a colored triangle to be sewn onto their uniforms. Dirk was given a red one along with the man who was beaten, while the other two prisoners were given green ones. They were then led out of the building. Dirk and his fellow "red" prisoner were separated from the "green" prisoners and led to a barracks where they were assigned a bunk. They were to be quarantined for three weeks before being reassigned to a permanent barracks.

Dirk made a point of asking his companion what had happened to him during interrogation by the Gestapo. The man responded, "I was caught putting a poster up on a wall downtown in Munich that was not very complimentary of Adolph. They were trying to find out whether or not I was acting alone or part of a larger group. So far, I haven't given them any information about who I work with on our pamphlet project.

"I've been beaten by the police before, and the one I got this time was fairly mild. I don't know whether I will be able to hold out, though, if they torture me. They know that I'm a communist anyway, so I imagine they have some idea of who my friends are. They told me that I would be interrogated further here at Dachau."

Dirk placed his bags under the bunk and said, "Well, we're evidently going to have to both pay some sort of price for our feelings about the Nazis." Dirk soon found out that he had been designated a political prisoner and that he would eventually be sent to a portion of the camp reserved for political prisoners. Conditions were sometimes better for a political prisoner than for some of the other prisoner categories and especially better than those marked with yellow triangles. That color was for Jews. The two other prisoners who had traveled from Munich were given green triangles, which classified them as common criminals. They were separated and led to another part of the huge camp complex.

Dirk found that the prisoners actually did the administration of the interior of the camp and the most powerful of the various prisoner categories were the criminals and the political ones. The SS established and supervised the prisoner administration and, in most cases, let it run the camp interior without much interference.

The prisoners had a pecking order and they turned somersaults trying to endear themselves to the Totenkopf or Death's Head guard detachment. The prisoners had almost a complete organization among themselves governing the inside of the camp. The criminal element tried to dominate and there were constant clashes between the "reds" and the "greens" — sometimes violent. There was a constant threat of bullying from the tougher members of these two groups who had managed to ingratiate themselves to the guards and had more freedom than the others. But the political prisoners were also numerous and strong. Dirk decided soon after his arrival that he would do his best to maintain an invisible presence as much as possible to the SS guards as well as to the prisoners who ran the interior administration and had garnered their favor.

Josef Becomes a Confidant

Josef and Frieda began to meet regularly to discuss Dirk and attempt to understand what was happening in his life. It would be a long time before more detailed information came to light. Until then, there were only a few rumors and speculations coming from the camps. For the most part, German people themselves were closemouthed. The allies used counterintelligence; some of their findings sifted to a select few. Frieda's cohorts in leafleting picked up some intelligence information.

Dirk's absence created a void for both Josef and Frieda. The time they had spent with Dirk was now empty. The social activities, the dinners, the plays, and the musical events had come to an end. Dirk had been a best friend to both of them. Frieda missed Dirk's closeness, both emotionally and physically

As for Josef, men have their own interests. He and Dirk enjoyed skiing and hiking the Bavarian Alps. Outdoor activities were important to people living in proximity to such a beautiful landscape. They were among the experts and, in fact, Josef was a ski instructor as well as a guide for parties hiking the Alps.

Frieda and Josef's companionship strengthened. They took on some of the activities previously enjoyed with Dirk. Their bond remained with Dirk, however.

In such circumstances, where and when do emotions align with someone new? They shared the deep loss and grief of a friend. Their importance to one another was a subtle change with both being unaware of what was happening to their emotions.

As Frieda had written to her parents, during time of war

or impending war, people tended to latch on to relationships without question of what they might become in the future. It was a time when people needed other people that they could trust. A trusting relationship pushed away fears and made life normal once again.

They were both dancing on the edge of a new reality. What they were to do with this reality was still uncertain.

Keeping her feet on the ground wasn't easy. Frieda had experienced many changes within the past months. She needed to be with Aunt Grace who was, above all, a comforter. Aunt Grace listened without placing blame, expressing an opinion only when asked to do so.

Tearfully, Frieda spilled her story. "Aunt Grace, we have enjoyed each other's company since I arrived here. What I have not mentioned to you earlier, I would like to tell you now. The love of my life, Professor Dirk de Vries, has been arrested and taken away by the military police. There has been a letter from him from Dachau. He is still alive and works in a factory, pending a trial. I can only guess that the factory is in Dachau, close to the concentration camp."

"My dear Frieda, I'm so sorry that you are experiencing Germany in such a painful way. Nothing is the same for any of us. To have your first love abruptly ended is almost unthinkable. I know there is no justice, no fighting back that can make this right again," Aunt Grace said in a soothing voice.

Frieda continued, "Dirk was a professor at the university; he had many young admiring students. Dirk's lectures carried a subtle message of satire concerning Nazism. He had obviously reached many people with his message of opposition to the Nazi war machine."

Aunt Grace commented, "Such courage seems to have been a dangerous thing for him to have shown."

"I love him dearly, Aunt Grace; I'm destined to remain in Germany pending his trial and the outcome of the trial. It's timely that the leafleting should be strengthened and continued," Frieda noted.

"Frieda, you're giving me information about your lover's arrest. Why does it not surprise me that you are choosing now to let me know about your activities in leafleting? Sometimes the less we know, the better off we are. I was aware that with Hans' helping hand you were involved in some kind of political action, but I never ventured to guess what that might be," Aunt Grace said.

Frieda had not wanted to burden her aunt with this information; however, she felt that her own stress had been lightened after having confided in her.

As Frieda said goodbye to Aunt Grace, she thanked her for her willingness to listen and comfort her.

Aunt Grace cautioned Frieda, "For your own good, heed my warning that you must be very careful. Do not allow yourself to be linked with your Professor Dirk or any anti-Hitler activities."

Both expressed their love for one another as Frieda left the home of her aunt and uncle. Frieda paused to convey her love to her uncle, as well.

～❧

Life according to Aunt Grace gave Frieda a unique understanding of Germany. Her aunt was proud to be a genuine child of Munich. There were few left in the city; many were immigrants from cities and villages from the countryside looking for work. Unemployment was evident throughout Germany. Hitler built the autobahn to help get rid of unemployment. Aunt Grace saw the autobahn as a precursor to militarization of Germany. Road builders were paid 50 cents an hour for hard labor.

She spoke of Hitler before he came to power, positive that it would lead to war. Aunt Grace was suspicious of Hitler's promises to improve life for the German people. Most Nazi supporters were of the middle class. Many had good positions working in offices, and because of good jobs, they didn't have to leave to go to war. So only the dumb ones had to fight the war, Aunt Grace concluded.

The mid to late 1930s was a time of relative prosperity for many Germans. However, beginning in 1939, the German people began to live with blackout measures and other wartime restrictions. It was necessary to stay home after dusk. Food was rationed and ration cards had to be used. Those with Nazi contacts had good jobs and more food.

The German people grumbled about the blackouts and time spent dealing with restrictions. News came of the outbreak of the war when Germans crossed Polish borders on September 3, 1939. Two days later, Britain and France declared war on Germany. Germans did not complain about their own government's role in the blackouts. Blame was placed on Poland, Britain, and France.

For the most part, Jews with money had left Germany by 1938. They had sensed what was coming and emigrated to America or elsewhere. Prior to the outbreak of the war, SS Administrators, under the leadership of Adolph Eichmann, were given the task of facilitating the departure of as many Jews as possible through emigration. When war was declared, the emigration program was stopped. Jews were no longer permitted to leave for countries outside of the German sphere. Jews began to be deported to the East into ghettos and concentration camps in Poland.

Closing In

Frieda's friends in the leafleting activities did not meet regularly. Upon arriving at Frieda's flat, Rose, a member of the group, knocked at her door. Over coffee, Rose commented, "The birds are migrating." Frieda recognized it as a code phrase indicating that their group, responsible for the leaflet writing and distribution, was greatly at risk for detection by the Gestapo.

Frieda assessed her situation and made a plan to quietly close out her business. There was no further need for leaflets. She decided to go to Aunt Grace and tell her that her life had changed.

"Aunt Grace, we have always known that our leaflet distribution was risky. I'm afraid we have gone too long and too far," Frieda said with a fearful note.

"My dear, Frieda, I don't want to know any details. It's best to leave such things unsaid," Aunt Grace commented. "You are an American citizen with a passport. You know what you must do next."

"It will be soon, Aunt Grace. If I should not see you before I leave, please know that you and Uncle Karl have been my only family. I love both of you dearly and thank you for all that you have done for me," Frieda said tearfully.

As she was leaving, Uncle Karl, home from work, greeted her. Frieda hurriedly explained that she would be leaving Germany soon and was happy that he should be there when she was saying goodbye. Uncle Karl showed his emotions with a hug and wished her well.

Keeping her own tears on hold, Aunt Grace hugged Frieda,

asking if there was anything else that she could do. Frieda did ask for one more thing. She asked her to arrange another meeting with the Spider.

~⌐

Frieda met the Spider the next day. She said, "Hans, I just want to let you know that we no longer need your help. We so appreciate what you have done for us in making our leafleting work longer and farther. But it seems that things are coming to a head here. What we are doing is a lost cause, and we can only hope that the United States will enter the war soon."

The Spider said, "Fraulein, my sources tell me that the Gestapo is close on your heels. Before you leave the country, I would like to provide a connector to another phase of the war against the Nazis. These operations, too, are necessary."

Frieda replied, "I've lived on the edge during my time in Germany. At this time, closure should not come as a surprise; however, emotionally I am not ready. I have experienced a personal loss. Although the outcome of the arrest of Professor de Vries remains unknown, I feel as though I am abandoning him if I should leave here."

"Fraulein, you must leave. Sacrificing your own life will only strengthen the Nazi war machine. You must continue the fight. Opposition is necessary. I am giving you a unique opportunity. When I explain this to you, I hope that you will accept this offer immediately and allow me to set in motion plans for your safe and immediate departure to America," Hans said.

Hans continued to lay out a future for Frieda. She would work with an arm of the U.S. Army that helped utilize intelligence from foreign sources in Washington, D.C. Women were needed in this service because men assigned there had been drafted into active service in the military. She would be given time to travel home to Philadelphia for rest and relaxation before reporting to Army headquarters in Washington.

Frieda mentally assessed her situation. Bridges had been burned behind her. She needed direction for a new future; she felt complimented with the offer to work for Armed Services in Washington. It was close to her home in Philadelphia: close to her parents and all those things that were of comfort to her.

However, she did not want to be too comfortable while others were suffering deeply. America, too, would experience many changes when it entered the war. The world, as Frieda knew it, was shaken.

"Hans, right now I'm looking at you as my lifeline. It seems that I've no road to travel. Please try and get me passage to my next assignment. I have only Josef, Professor de Vries' best friend, to contact before I leave Germany. He would be most interested in knowing my whereabouts. However, it may be safer to do that by letter after I return to Philadelphia. Right now, I put my life in your hands and will follow your lead for my safety," Frieda said calmly.

"Fraulein, do not return to your flat. I'll have your basic belongings packed in one suitcase and taken to a safe house. Here is the address where I want you to go after this meeting," Hans informed her.

Frieda Sails Away from Germany

The Spider lived up to his promises and soon had made arrangements for Frieda's departure. She was spirited out of Germany in a disguise and was driven across the Spanish frontier by one of his contacts. From there, she was taken to Portugal and then to England. She boarded an American merchant marine vessel and began her slow voyage back to her homeland. Frieda spent many hours reviewing what had happened to her as the ship slowly sailed westward through the Atlantic. She also thought about her home and of times past and how important they were to her growth from a child into an adult.

Frieda's fondest childhood memories were of her parents and the stately Victorian house on a quiet street in Philadelphia. Father was a physician; Mother was a straight-laced modern woman working with other Quakers to bring social justice for women, children, the poor, the uneducated, and the imprisoned. This made for an interesting home life; the discussions at dinner were all about issues. Some people talk about trivia, while others discuss issues. Frieda considered herself fortunate. She had a mind like her parents.

Father and Mother were evenly yoked. Father practiced medicine; Mother worked with the Quaker movement to bring change and improve the quality of life for the majority who fell between the cracks. Lawmakers and men in general dominated the state of affairs existing at that time. Frieda had a happier home life because Father was a doctor devoted to healing and kindness. Mother didn't have to convert him to an understanding and compassion for the underdog.

In those days, many wives were considered to be no more than chattels, incapable of understanding business. A good wife knew only about things of the home, child rearing, and maintaining a social standing. Such a woman first had to weasel a way to convince her husband that she sincerely wanted to work with other women to bring about social change. She must show him that change was needed and persuade her husband that her responsibilities at home, her duty to her husband and children, wouldn't be thwarted in any way.

Little Eva made her home with Frieda and her parents and, as a child, Frieda once said, "Little Eva, you're my very best friend."

"Little" was a title of endearment that was also descriptive of the woman herself. For Frieda, Little Eva had always been there and was a part of the household. Little Eva had been an orphan and was brought into the family home when she was a young girl. She was reared by Frieda's parents and continued to live with them into her adulthood. She was a small, slight person made matronly and dignified by a pullback hairstyle and Oxford shoes. The shoes were made sturdy with one-and-a-half-inch thick heels. Her simple appearance was not unlike mother's. Fashion was not that important and would have been a distraction to faith and Christian duty.

Little Eva's natural place in the home was helping mother make sure that the household ran smoothly. She was the adult companion to Frieda in her childhood and during the years she grew into a young lady.

"Look at what I can do," Frieda once called out to Little Eva. "See, I'm flying down the stairs." Sliding down the banister on her stomach with her feet barely touching the steps was one of Frieda's favorite things to do. Practiced frequently, she was so skilled at stair flying that it continued in her dreams into adulthood. In her dreams she was actually flying down the stairs without her feet touching.

"Little Eva, I'm good at flying around the room above your head, but you can't see me do it," Frieda confided.

"My, you have an active imagination, Frieda," Little Eva commented.

"But Eva, I can really do it. It's just that no one can see me do it," Frieda said.

Eva replied, "Young lady, exactly how do you fly around a room at the ceiling?"

Frieda explained, "I breathe just right, first beginning by holding my breath, and then I hold that breath in my body in a certain way until my body lifts and I'm flying."

Somewhat fascinated, Eva asked, "And what do you see while floating and zooming around a room?"

Pleased that she was finally being heard, Frieda said, "Sometimes there are some people, but they can't see me. I'm speaking with my thoughts, saying, look at me, see what I can do."

In fact, Frieda would never acknowledge that her practice of levitation and flying continued into adulthood. It was just there, giving her delightful dreams. One day, later in life, she analyzed the dreams and decided that she could not possibly fly. That was the end of the dreams. No more flying, no more sliding down the staircase with feet not touching. In her dreams, nothing had touched.

Levitation and stair flying were Frieda's pastimes indoors; visiting her grandparents on the farm came in as a third pleasurable interest. She loved lying in the grass and dreaming. Frieda was planning and making her own future. She would be a famous and influential writer one day. The breeze gently touched her skin and hair. Light of heart, Frieda lifted her skirts above her knees and danced.

And so, on a late autumn day in 1940, Frieda disembarked from her ship in New York, made her way to the railroad station, and caught a train to Philadelphia. A taxi took her through familiar streets to her parent's house. Approaching the lovely Victorian home, Frieda first gave attention to the grass growing in a Y-shaped piece defined by the sidewalk intersecting. As a child she had identified plantain, imagining that it was lettuce. She once made imaginary salads for playtime with her dolls. As she walked up the sidewalk and near to the door, she sobbed uncontrollably. She had not planned to show emotion; the disciplined household of her childhood was bereft of extreme feelings and behavior.

Frieda's mother and father embraced her with joy. Frieda felt as though she had been in a desert, lacking abundant love and security. It was only in Germany that Frieda had painful experiences; before, the pain would have been cushioned by her parents. Little Eva stepped to the forefront, giving Frieda a hug.

"My goodness, girl, you have finally come home to us. You're a woman now. I believe I see dark circles around your eyes and sadness in your face," noted Little Eva.

"Dear ones, I do feel fortunate to have escaped Germany and to be alive. There is so much happening there; many things I'm sure you don't know about. The world news in America is not keeping up with the events," said Frieda.

Mother said, "Come, we must first give Frieda some food and make her comfortable."

After a magnificent dinner, Frieda changed out of her travel clothes to join her family in the drawing room. It was a formal room; but it was very comfortable. Frieda could now appreciate the room as an adult. As a child she had felt overwhelmed with the Victorian furnishings. She remembered her feet dangling over the sofa, legs too short to reach the floor. She had not been away very long; however, she now saw with new eyes the home where she had grown up.

Father began the conversation, "Frieda, when your mother and I agreed to send you to Germany to complete your studies, we had no idea of the political change that country was undergoing. We had the very best intentions and were confident that you would find protection with Uncle Karl and Aunt Grace."

Frieda replied, "Uncle Karl and Aunt Grace were wonderful. They kept me secure in their home, treating me as a member of their family. Eventually I chose to strike out on my own and found a flat near the university."

"As I wrote to you earlier, I fell in love with a young professor. I attended his open lectures and listened to political satire about National Socialism. He was one of many professors arrested for failing to embrace Nazi propaganda and the new order being brought about," Frieda sobbed as the story spilled.

Mother held Frieda in her arms, "I'm so sorry for your pain, my dear."

Frieda said, "Dirk's best friend, Josef, received a letter from Dirk in Dachau saying that he was working in a factory while awaiting trial. Then we heard nothing further. The only information that we had was that many were executed without a trial, depending on the crime."

Seeing how distraught his daughter was, Father suggested that they all go to bed and continue their talks the next day.

Frieda awoke to a knock on her door. Little Eva announced that breakfast was ready and the family was waiting for her. She dressed quickly and met them in the breakfast room. She was drawn to the smell of bacon cooking and muffins baking. Sunshine coming through the windows showed off the arrangement of fresh flowers in the center of the table. Yes, it certainly was good to be home.

After breakfast, they began talking about Hitler and how he seemed to be a threat to all of Europe. Hitler had taken control of Austria, Poland, Belgium, France, the Netherlands, Denmark, Norway, and Czechoslovakia. Father said, "You are right, Frieda. Americans do not understand how Europe is changing. There is a great distance and an ocean between America and Europe. The most news is coming from radio. Newscasts have become more prominent; they now focus on war rather than entertainment."

Mother commented, "Right now it seems that British Prime Minister Churchill is hoping that we will eventually get into the war and help them defeat Germany. I think that President Roosevelt is preparing us to go to war with Germany, and it won't be too long before it happens."

"Power is necessary to combat the Nazi war machine. I can tell you firsthand, the world will never be the same again. There are concentration camps, basic freedoms have been taken away, and people spy upon one another. They trust no one," Frieda responded emotionally.

Father observed, "In his speeches on radio, Edward R. Murrow, a correspondent for CBS, has brought us news of the war crisis in Europe. He has kept us pretty well up-to-date on what is going on if people want to really find out about it. Murrow is the first to bring coverage of Europe. We are now informed, and knowledge of the situation has reached America."

"I like to listen to President Roosevelt's program, *Fireside Chats*. Imagine remote farm home families sitting around the radio expecting information that might offer hope. The Great Depression affects all of us, some more than others. President Roosevelt's chats are warm and full of positive thoughts of the future," Little Eva said with tears in her eyes.

During the course of Frieda's stay with her family, she gained courage to confide in them about her resistance against the Nazi war machine.

"Mother, it's from you that I have learned to be courageous and a fighter for justice. Non-violent resistance makes a strong statement against intense aggression," ventured Frieda.

"Frieda, I want you to feel free to discuss these activities with us. You are safe in our country now. Secrecy is no longer necessary," Father encouraged.

Frieda began the story that could have ended in her arrest. "I want to tell you briefly about leafleting in which I actively participated. After Dirk was arrested and taken to Dachau, I was frantic and struck out in anger against Hitler's National Socialism. I joined a group, writing and distributing anti-Nazi leaflets. It was a dangerous thing to do, and we all knew it. But we were so angry, we ignored the danger."

Little Eva asked, "And what happened next, Frieda?"

"I was asked to become business manager for the group and the leaflet efforts. Keeping records of income and expenses was left to me. At first, funding came from families; later, we wanted to expand distribution of leaflets. We needed more money for supplies. Help came unexpectedly and when we desperately needed it. Little miracles do happen," Frieda recalled.

Frieda continued, "I was sitting on a park bench near the university one day, and a stranger struck up a conversation. It seems that he is a neighbor of Uncle Karl and Aunt Grace. He introduced himself as Hans; however, I'll always remember him as the Spider who sat down beside me on the park bench. His limbs were gangly and uncoordinated, reminding me of a spider."

"I was suspicious, not knowing where his political allegiance might lie. It crossed my mind that he might be Gestapo.

He offered us money for any effort that we may undertake. After considering his rather strange offer, I decided to trust him. He would not acknowledge that he was with the Allies, however, my decision to place my trust in him was one of the best that I could have made," Frieda explained.

Father said, "Frieda, had we known that you were risking yourself, we certainly would have arranged to bring you home."

"The Spider and I met on three occasions, each time he brought money in an envelope. I began to wear a disguise for our meetings so I wouldn't be recognized if I was being followed. Surveillance is most common in Germany today," Frieda commented.

Frieda continued, "I met with the Spider one more time to thank him for his help. Our work with the leaflet program appeared to make little difference against the Nazi war machine. We were losing ground. Spider told me that he was aware of the situation, and according to his sources, the Gestapo was close on my heels. He said that I must leave Germany at once, and that he would arrange for me to have safe passage. He instructed me not to return to my flat. He said he would have my basic belongings packed in a single suitcase; he handed me an address where I was to go immediately and await passage to America."

They were all exhausted from hearing the hair-raising story Frieda had just shared with them. Frieda said good night, knowing that her parents and Little Eva would have more questions tomorrow. Now it was time to write Josef in Germany and explain herself. She must keep in mind that Josef's mail would be censored.

My dear Josef,

I am now in America, safe with my parents and family. It became necessary for me to leave Germany for my own security; my American passport gave safe passage. Continuing studies at the university had become impossible; the other circumstances of which you know, gave little reason for me to stay in Germany. My thoughts are drawn to both you and our friend Dirk.

My very best wishes,
(Signed) Frieda

The American Army Arrives

When the American Army finally arrived in Germany after years of war, they were assigned areas by the Supreme Commander of Allied Forces. The American Army was operational in a portion of southern Germany. The population was partly hostile and yet glad that the end of the violence and air raids had at last come. In some places, the U.S. Army demonstrated by individual actions that it was willing to be a goodwill ambassador and help the population when it could.

Near one village, for instance, a German boy, about four years of age, fell face down in a stream and was in danger of drowning. A ham-like black hand reached down and grabbed the clothes on his back, pulling the child to his feet and to safety. An American soldier had made a dramatic rescue as the Army made its appearance in the rural villages it passed through during its invasion. It was the boy's first introduction to the American army, and he did not forget.

The Allies occupied Cologne, Germany, on March 6, 1945. The boy's rescue from drowning took place in the area of the Bavarian Alps south of Cologne shortly thereafter. The child had been chasing a chicken, running beyond the watchfulness of his mother. The child knew how precious a chicken was for producing eggs, for he knew all about hunger.

Families, usually mothers and children, had fled the cities for safer places. Fathers were fighting in the war. The influx of people meant that local households must absorb additional people. It also meant that schools must do the same. Classrooms of 20 or 30 expanded to accommodate again as many students. Teachers were often elderly men; young male teachers were now soldiers.

Along with the American Army came food for the schoolchildren. The Marshall Plan was responsible for feeding the many people whose lives had been uprooted. About one third of the population were refugees, many from East Prussia. Each household took two or three refugees into their homes. It was mandated by law that the refugees should be integrated into the populace in this way.

Schoolchildren were made to share food they received in school; families instructed the children to bring half home for younger siblings. Somehow these bittersweet childhood memories lasted a lifetime.

Uncle Karl and Aunt Grace had fled their home in Munich, taking refuge in the Bavarian Alps. Uncle Karl served as a physician to the people in communities expanded with refugees. Aunt Grace was called upon to be a nurse, giving her ample opportunity to pass along both professional and homespun advice. She found this very satisfying; she felt needed. Her work became a distraction. Leaving one's home and belongings is difficult for women. They have spent a lifetime cleaning, cooking, and maintaining their home. Aunt Grace, like all Germans, felt it important to take care of what belongs to them.

Discussing their current situation, Aunt Grace told Uncle Karl, "I'm so happy that Frieda returned to America when she did. There would have been no place for her here. One must be German to face being displaced and knowing that so many have little food."

Uncle Karl said, "We must write Frieda and her family to let them know where we are and what we are doing."

Frieda Goes to Washington

Frieda climbed the open spiral staircase of the Victorian house in a Washington, D.C., neighborhood. She had just picked up a key to the second floor apartment that was to be her home. She unlocked the door and took a quick look around. It was very small; however, she felt fortunate to have a place to call her own.

The kitchenette was tiny with no room for a kitchen sink. Rather it had a small bathroom-sized lavatory sink. At the perimeter of the living room were a small sofa, lamp and table, and side chair, all scaled down to suit the room. The center of the room was uncluttered until which time the Murphy bed was pulled down. The bed took up almost every available space. There was some natural light coming from a small window in the living room. She would find that dust and debris collected on the wide windowsill in the bathroom.

As the Spider had told her, Frieda was enlisted in the Military Intelligence section of the U.S. Army in Washington, D.C., after a number of months of rest with her parents in Philadelphia. With the men overseas, the U.S. Government recruited women as "government girls" to fill the vacated positions. Frieda joined this force of temporary workers who were hired only for the duration of the national emergency. The collection of recruits came as a result of newspaper and magazine ads placed cautiously. Recruiting was a challenge since there could be very little explanation about the work itself. Many of the recruits for this Army unit were without skills. Those who were educated in a specific profession were quickly grabbed up to be assigned to the various activities and branches of the Intelligence Unit. Frieda's language skills were to give her opportunities that the majority of the employees would never see.

Women and men who served in the Intelligence Unit were ordered to keep their work secret. If asked what they did, they were to reply that they were clerks; clerical work was somewhat mundane and would not lead to further questions.

With lingering pain and memories, Frieda now turned to a new life. The shortage of affordable housing for a single government worker was everywhere. Women of importance working for the government could afford hotel rooms and more luxurious accommodations. Homeowners in Washington and the environs were asked to rent extra space in their homes to the influx of government workers. This space was often little more than a closet with a bed and the cost of rent was exorbitant.

However, Frieda had a very influential contact in the Spider. Not only had he arranged for her work, he also pulled strings to obtain a suitable apartment for her. Spider had great expectations for Frieda and her educated approach to writing. Her experience in Munich writing anti-Nazi leaflets would become a precursor to any new assignments she might be given working for the U.S.

～⌒

Soon after getting settled into her Washington apartment, Frieda visited her landlady, Mrs. Landau, to get acquainted and become oriented to her new surroundings. This was a safe place for young women who were living alone.

Mrs. Landau said, "Frieda, welcome to my home. The house is divided into four small apartments, all occupied by young women. I live alone on the first floor and am here most of the time. I do, of course, run errands and occasionally visit friends. If you should need anything, just knock at my door. I want all of my young ladies to feel secure and happy here."

"I can't tell you how pleased I am with the apartment and with having my own privacy. I read a great deal and do some cooking. I noticed a small grocery several blocks away. It's possible to shop without taking a bus," she said.

"As for laundry, there is a wringer-washer and clothes line

in the basement. I find that many of my tenants have never done laundry. In fact, I recently had to remove a sheet that someone inept had inadvertently allowed to wrap around the wringer. It took all my strength to release it," said Mrs. Landau.

Frieda could visualize the strong, tall, large-boned woman pulling on the sheet that had wrapped tightly around two rollers. Yes, she thought to herself, the sheet most certainly had to give.

Frieda noted, "The bus stop at the end of the block is very convenient."

During the conversation, Mrs. Landau added one more bit of information. "I'll tell you, as I have told all my residents, young gentleman callers are not welcome here. The telephone in the foyer is for emergency use only; there will be no lengthy conversations held in the foyer."

Incidents occurred that would stick in Frieda's mind. The little grocery store close by often became a stage for those who wished to notice the various life dramas nearby. A mother with a three or four-year-old daughter stopped Frieda one day and asked for money to buy food for the little girl. Frieda herself was short of funds; she had not yet worked nor been paid. The woman was simply and neatly dressed. Frieda was one not to be taken advantage of; however, she felt compassion. She gave the woman a quarter. Frieda again crossed paths with the woman and child in the store and noted that the mother was carrying an orange and one egg. That's what a quarter would buy as a meal for one small child.

Frieda snuggled into her warm bed feeling thankful for simple comforts. She had just finished a bowl of hot soup that she had cooked; the lingering aroma filled her apartment. Tomorrow she would report to work for the Army.

∾

Frieda reported to the Commanding Officer of the Military Intelligence Section of the Army for a briefing. She soon learned that these were black operations. Although it was against her conscience to participate in such efforts, she had only to remember Dirk, the man who was missing from her life. She had deliberately decided to take his name, de Vries, as her own, and had formally changed it officially through the courts of the Commonwealth of Pennsylvania. The name change somehow gave her a comforting feeling that her ties would someday be renewed. But Dirk was not there in the here and now and life had to go on without him.

Frieda, as well as many who were recruited to work for the Army, was not instantly sold on being under the thumb of rigid authority. Many were just out of college and were lured into serving their country even before they could seek a profession. For those who wore uniforms, they often appeared to be limp and lacking starch. So, in the months that followed, Frieda became a busy employee of the U.S. Army Intelligence Unit in Washington.

Sometime in 1941, President Roosevelt felt that there was a very great need for a special organization designed to gather intelligence instead of the job being spread out in the various military branches of the War Department. There was too much duplication of services and agency strife for such an important task to continue in such a haphazard manner. William Joseph Donovan came to the attention of the President and in July of 1941, the President appointed him as Coordinator of Information and he began to consolidate the various U.S. intelligence-gathering efforts into a newly formed organization. He became the director of the unit.

As 1942 came and the European war intensified, President Roosevelt asked Donovan to put together the framework for a new organization to serve the needs of intelligence gathering, spying, and secret work aimed at defeating Nazi Germany. Donovan was tasked with setting up what was called the Office of Strategic Services or OSS. He set in place operations for the purpose of using deception and subversion to undermine belief in Hitler and Nazism. Donovan had seen the effectiveness of Nazi propaganda and saw the importance of similar operations for the United States. Frieda and the other employees of the Army Intelligence Unit were absorbed into the organization that Donovan birthed.

Frieda was called into the commanding officer's office one day and told that she and a large number of other employees were to be transferred to a new organization. This new organization would be doing all that the Intelligence Unit had been doing and more. Her transfer followed shortly in September of 1941, and she began work in another building set up to house the organization. For the time being, her work with the Coordinator of Intelligence was similar to what she had been doing with the Army, but after several weeks, she was asked to sit in with other employees for a briefing on a new branch of the OSS in which she would work and which was being set up. Frieda was to become part of the Morale Branch.

~~~

When the OSS was finally organized, Frieda participated in the overseas indoctrination held at special training schools in Washington, Maryland, and Virginia. Qualified candidates received training to organize and manipulate resistance groups, engage in espionage, initiate whisper campaigns, make counterfeit documents, sabotage rail bridges, and penetrate enemy lines. Considered to be legal, all must be done without getting caught.

Frieda's training for writing black propaganda was described as mixing detailed truth with believable lies. Women generally were found to be very good at this craft. Frieda would find that after spending many months in intelligence work where she hid the truth, slanted stories, and developed rumors, she would later have great difficulty in writing a straight story. But time passed and general war in Europe finally broke out. The United States declared war on Germany in December 1941 after several years of sending needed supplies to Great Britain. The attack on Pearl Harbor opened a second front for the United States. The invasion of Russia by Germany brought even more urgency to what Frieda was doing. Psychological warfare became a much-needed part of the hot war that was now in full swing. Most of Europe was occupied by Hitler or allied with him against Russia, Great Britain, and the United States.

Frieda worked at first with the publication and campaign division that was responsible for producing leaflets, pamphlets, and whispering campaigns. Frieda was best suited for this work, although she would find movement within the OSS in the future. For instance, she also worked with the Special

Communications Detachment, which produced and dissemi-
nated combat propaganda in coordination with the U.S. Army
in Europe.

The OSS staff was not allowed to keep diaries; consequently, as time went by, the details of what they did exactly
were often forgotten. Black propaganda was part of the effort to
carry out psychological warfare operations for the U.S. Army.
The Morale Operations Branch had outposts located around the
globe near U.S. Army combat stations or they were integrated
into Army intelligence posts. By the end of the war in Europe
in 1945, there were stations in London, Britain, Italy, Algeria,
Egypt, France, and Sweden.

The time she spent in Germany and the work she did in
resistance gave Frieda the experience needed to succeed in the
OSS. Knowing the German language and having gone to school
in Germany were important qualifying credentials. Much of
the work required knowledge and use of European, Arabic, or
Asian languages. People with skills such as math, cartography,
and cryptography were also sought.

In retrospect, the OSS pulled together a workforce whose
members learned to apply their knowledge, skills, and apti-
tude. These people had not been taught in schools for a career
in Secret Service work, but rather they had come from the grass
roots of the United States with various skill and educational
levels. The workforce was built quickly; some received more
training than others, and what they shared was enthusiasm for
the work ahead. Several years before OSS agents worked in the
war zones of Europe, covert operations were being developed
in New York City. Women were recruited worldwide for OSS
activities centering in New York City.

A major leafleting program was now part of the OSS efforts
and Frieda, with her earlier experience, became involved in it.
Leaflets were prepared in Washington and distributed to the
European theater. Recorded in history, the first black leaflet
campaign was known as How Much Longer? There was a series
of 16 leaflets depicting cartoon figures asking how much longer
the German people could tolerate their current difficult situation. Leaflets were distributed throughout southern France,
Italy, and the Balkans.

Each day, Frieda took the bus back to her apartment. Each day she was exhausted from all of the new experiences, knowing that she had a great deal to learn and remember. Food shopping and cooking were relaxing and provided diversion. Cleaning up the kitchen was not easy, especially with the miniature sink. The dining table was in the other room that served as living room and bedroom. She sat at the small, drop-leaf table, reading the newspaper as she ate. She did not even miss having a companion to share the meals; it was so good to relax.

After a meal, Frieda went for a walk around the neighborhood. It was a neighborhood of Victorian houses much like the one where she lived. It was good to get fresh air and some exercise. This always prepared her for doing some reading before she went to bed. There is something comforting about an established routine. She must give thought to building another book collection; it had been necessary to leave behind in Germany some of her favorite literature, history, and travel books.

One day, Mrs. Landau was in the foyer to greet Frieda as she came in from work. She said, "I've heard warnings that the city is undergoing a blackout this evening. Perhaps you have been briefed on that, but I wanted you to know so that you can prepare for it. Leaving your apartment is probably not a good thing. Being caught downtown or anywhere would be confusing in pitch darkness.

Frieda replied, "We were told that this might happen, but details for what this really means to us were not discussed. A blackout in Washington is something that I had never thought about. After leaving Germany, I hoped not to encounter such things again."

The next day at work, people were discussing where they were and what they had been doing when the blackout took place. Two of the young women were to meet outside a hotel in downtown Washington before going to the home of another friend. It was too dark to find their way and a warden patrolling the area helped them by giving directions.

Frieda was beginning to understand that offices and operations were compartmentalized. At lunchtime, they crossed the lines and chatted while waiting in line at the cafeteria. The girls shared rationed food and an abundance of coffee that was freely available. Frieda learned that some had received orders to London, Algiers, Bern, and Istanbul. The girls remaining in the offices wrote reports and initiated propaganda that had originated from enemy sources. Others learned to forge documents and master cryptography.

Skorpion West was another famed leaflet campaign. The German propaganda team out of France created optimistic leaflets to boost morale. The leaflets were airdropped across the line to bolster the spirits of the German soldiers. The OSS Morale Operations obtained copies of the leaflets and produced facsimiles. The Germans believed that the false documents were genuine and distributed them. The facsimile leaflets produced by OSS were in three parts and meant to create chaos.

1. The German high command felt that their soldiers would be unable to hold the line and suggested that they should burn everything in sight before dying, in a last stand for National Socialism.

2. The second pamphlet ordered all soldiers to shoot any officers who attempted to surrender or retreat.

3. The third pamphlet ordered soldiers to carry out evacuation of civilians by force. (The allies hoped that this would clog traffic and supply lines.)

Eventually the Germans denounced all Skorpion West pamphlets, including the ones their own propaganda team had created and ordered all troops to ignore their messages.

Delivering Leaflet Propaganda

Leaflet bombs dropped from aircraft delivered tens of thousands of leaflets in strategic areas. For the Americans, the first such bomb was developed from laminated paper containers that had been used to transport incendiary bombs. It was implemented in 1943 by the American military. At a predetermined time, the two halves of the bombs' outer shell were blown apart by a detonating cord, dispersing the leaflets. Such a bomb often contained 60,000 to 80,000 leaflets.

Leaflet disbursement was handled somewhat differently by the Germans and British. The British used hydrogen balloons to carry leaflets over German lines. On the other hand, the Germans launched their own bombs against Southern England. The leaflets were contained in a cardboard tube at the tail of a missile. The tube was ejected by a small, gunpowder charge while the plane was in mid-air and directed to its target.

After work Frieda and her co-workers rode buses home and took care of their own lives. Frieda enjoyed the chitchat in the cafeteria at work, but there were no close friendships formed mainly because of the secrecy concerning their work.

Mrs. Landau again greeted Frieda in the foyer as Frieda arrived from work. "I've invited my residents for a little social time about eight o'clock this evening. We all need to get to know one another better; I hope that you're able to come."

"What a nice surprise. It seems we must all be on different

schedules; I have not actually met the people living here. I look forward to coming," Frieda replied.

Frieda changed into more comfortable clothes, made dinner, and read the paper. She looked forward to a social time at Mrs. Landau's.

Shortly after eight o'clock she knocked at Mrs. Landau's door. The radio was playing cheerful background music, "Don't Sit Under the Apple Tree." Three other young women were there. Mrs. Landau introduced them to Frieda; they were all from Ohio—Evelyn, Esta, and Blanche.

As they chatted, Frieda learned that the three had known one another even before they came to Washington. Just out of high school, these girls decided to go to Washington for adventure and to do their patriotic duty. Rural Ohio residents were particularly known for their patriotism. Frieda could see that her own background was hugely different. Frieda had been in Germany and had lost her lover to Hitler. This was the driving force behind her own sense of patriotism for America.

Mrs. Landau was an admirable hostess with a knack for putting everyone at ease. She served fruit punch and a delicious cake. The chocolate mayonnaise cake was a favorite during the war. Mayonnaise replaced rationed items, both eggs and shortening. Food rationing brought a new wave of recipes where many traditional ingredients were substituted for another.

The conversation continued. It seemed that everyone employed in Washington was there for clerical duty. That was not surprising; it's what government workers were supposed to say to prevent further questioning. The five of them talked while the radio in the background played "Chattanooga Choo Choo" with the Glen Miller band.

Returning to her apartment, Frieda turned on the radio for the ten o'clock news. Commentator Edward R Murrow was reporting on the continuing blitz in London. The city of London was strategically bombed by the Germans. The bombing was reported beginning September 7, 1940 and continued for 76 consecutive nights. In London alone, more than 1 million houses were destroyed or damaged. More than 40,000 civilians were killed—half of them in London. Port cities were bombed. The important military and industrial city of Southampton was severely attacked, causing civilian authorities to move people out of the city.

Frieda listened to the radio news broadcasts daily. It connected her work in Washington with the European theater of war. She was fearful for her safety as far away as Washington, D.C., in America. She herself had come within a hair's width of death in Germany while carrying out anti-Hitler leafleting activities. She had only to remember her Dirk to know that being anti-Hitler was indeed playing with fire.

The next weekend, Frieda took time and thought to compose a letter to her parents. They would be interested in knowing what her life was like in Washington. Although they were not far away, Philadelphia seemed remote from where she was now living. Energies were high in Washington; there was a sense of dead seriousness and determination in the air. War in the European theater was indeed a severe challenge for Americans.

Dear Mother and Father,

It is time to sit down and have a chat. I wish you were here so that we could do this in person. Sometimes I feel that living with you both would be very comforting. The reality of living on my own during wartime is stark. I miss Dirk and the tenderness that he showed me. It is only love that helps us get by.

Washington is overflowing with government workers who came to take the positions of men who have been called to active duty. Housing is in short supply; especially housing that is affordable. I have managed to find a second-floor apartment in a Victorian house in a Washington, D.C., neighborhood. Three young women from Ohio live in the other three units. That makes four of us who share the house with Mrs. Landau, the owner and manager. She is like a housemother to us. We are not to have gentlemen callers nor use the telephone in the foyer, which is only for emergency purposes.

There is a small grocery store within walking distance. Cooking is a down to earth way of keeping my feet on the ground. One-dish meals are my favorites since the kitchen is very small, and the sink is a bathroom lavatory size. I sit at a drop-leaf table in the other room while eating and reading the paper. There is a sofa and in the center of the room is a Murphy bed. I think Murphy beds are a wonderful space saving concept. When pulled down from the wall, it takes up most of the room.

I listen to the news every evening, as I'm sure you do as well. Edward R. Murrow brings us the European news and we all follow Hitler's devastating movement throughout Europe. It is unimaginable to learn of the blitzing of London. Somehow London seems closer to the heart of Americans. Perhaps it is the English-language that binds us together.

As you know, I'm working daily on a job I can't really tell you about. We are not permitted to talk about or reveal what we do exactly. I can tell you only that my education and experience in writing have qualified me for important work.

Well, my dears, I'll bid you good night and look forward to a time when I may leave Washington for a weekend with you.

My love to you and Little Eva,
(Signed) Frieda

Having written and mailed the letter, Frieda felt warmth and love both to them and from them. It was a connection with the family who had great love and respect for one another.

The Morale Operations Branch introduced what was known as the Lichtenau Letter as part of their leaflet propaganda. The letter appeared to be a Christmas greeting from the Mayor of Lichtenau. It was first believed to be a morale booster for Nazi soldiers. Careful reading indicated that the letter included claims that government had drafted civilians into the military, and that young teenagers were becoming pilots after only a few weeks of training. It also implied that families back home sacrificed their health to promote the Nazi cause. This, along with other Nazi demoralizing leaflets, became part of documented history.

Frieda, as well as others working for OSS, realized that their effort was but a small piece of the puzzle. The big picture was obscure; it was meant to be clouded in mystery and secrecy. More explicit details about what was actually produced and carried out were documented after the war.

One of the greatest mysteries of World War II surprised most people including nearby residents. Spies, guerrilla leaders, and clandestine radio operators were trained in some of the national parks. The parks known as Catoctin Mountain Park in Maryland and Prince William Forest Park in Virginia were training sites for the operatives of the OSS. This military agency was fighting a largely invisible and covert war. The "shadow warriors" trained here, and then supplied and guided local resistance movements in Nazi Germany, Fascist Italy, and Japan.

The operatives hoped to demoralize the enemy through black propaganda. They gathered intelligence and sabotaged enemy-occupied territory. Those engaged in sabotage, blew up railroads, bridges, and tunnels. Other targets were power plants, communication centers, and weapons depots. Radio operators and members of the OSS Communications Branch kept field operatives and headquarters informed through encoded messages using shortwave radios and temporarily strung antennas. Operational groups infiltrated enemy lines in nighttime parachute drops and from submarines and small planes.

The vast majority of OSS personnel came from middle-class backgrounds. Selected on merit, they did a great deal of the work. There were also glamorous individuals from Hollywood and from the wealthiest families in America—the DuPonts, Mellons, Morgans, and Vanderbilts.

The OSS was a civilian wartime organization; many military personnel were assigned to it. It reported to the Joints Chiefs of Staff and the director, William J. Donovan, had personal access to President Franklin D. Roosevelt. In August 2008, the Central Intelligence Agency (CIA) released newly declassified OSS documents indicating that at one time, 24,000 people were employed by the OSS. The status of these 24,000 persons remains unclear as to whether they were permanent or temporary, consultant, American or foreign. From this organization stemmed some of the subsequent CIA directors.

Entertainment and Dancing

Chatting with the young women who had apartments in the same house, Frieda suggested that they all go dancing at the USO. The United Service Organization was a center for entertainment for the uniformed U.S. military. Yes, it was okay to dance with fellows you didn't know. Frieda, along with Evelyn, Esta, and Blanche, had the time of their lives, breaking the seriousness of their workdays. They found joy in the music, the gaiety, and the friendliness and laughter. It was pleasurable for Frieda, whose life had been filled with painful memories for a very long time. She thought back to times with Dirk. *No*, she thought, *it's time to live for today.*

Frieda and her three friends went to the USO center one evening a week, sometimes dancing, sometimes watching a movie. There were 160 centers worldwide whose concerns were morale, welfare, and recreational services for U.S. military personnel and their families. Spiritual services were made available and childcare allowed mothers time for relaxation. Some of the best-known entertainers in the world volunteered performances for troops at USO centers throughout the world.

President Roosevelt, the honorary chairman, brought six civilian organizations under one umbrella to support the U.S. troops. Roosevelt called upon private organizations to handle on-leave recreation of the men in the Armed Forces. Participating organizations were the Salvation Army, Young Men's Christian Association, Young Women's Christian Association, National Catholic Community Service, National Travelers Aid Association, and the National Jewish Welfare Board. The government was to build the buildings and the USO raised private funds to carry out its mission. The USO, although congressionally chartered, is not a government agency. It still continues today.

~~〜

Frieda, as well as all OSS personnel, was required to sign an oath of secrecy when she was recruited to work in the OSS shadow organization. The majority of women spent the war years at desks. They filed secret reports, encoded and decoded messages, and answered telephones. The intelligence division catalogued incoming material and forwarded it to the proper area. Dirty and dusty duffel bags of information came in from the European theater. The material had to be sorted and marked for distribution to the proper branches. The bags held information from underground agents.

Women assigned to covert operations were taught basic tradecraft such as breaking and entering, safe-blowing, and steaming letters open. The instructors were sometimes felons recruited to teach their trade.

Frieda was unaware of the details of the emotionally draining responsibilities of the majority of OSS employees. She knew only of her own; she was among those who went home at the end of the day hoping that at least their evening would be calm and settled. Of course there were some who dated young men and went to parties and dances. The seriousness of their work weighed heavily. However, youth was in their favor and they knew how to bring joy, fun, and happy times into their lives.

Mrs. Landau greeted Frieda in the foyer again one day. "Frieda, I'm inviting Evelyn, Esta, and Blanche for some music this evening. I know that you are an accomplished pianist. We would love to hear you play."

Frieda replied, "I'd like very much to come and play for you. We're all humming popular tunes these days. I'll see what I can come up with that everyone will know."

Frieda had recently stopped at a nearby music store for some sheet music. There were so many popular tunes that struck everyone's fancy. Under stress, Americans, like it or not, were fighting a war. Popular songs helped everyone get through it.

The music of World War II was so loved that it was to linger in people's minds for the rest of their lives.

Frieda and the other three young women enjoyed Mrs. Landau's motherly company and her apartment was warm, cozy, and welcoming. All the young women were reminded of their own home and their families.

Mrs. Landau greeted her guests at the door. "It's so good to see all of you. We have something special for this evening. Frieda will be playing the piano for us. On occasion I have heard her make the room rock with her playing."

"I just bought some new sheet music a few days ago," commented Frieda. "None of this actually rocks. In fact, I would say that it's somewhat melancholy."

Frieda sat down at the piano with everyone standing around looking over her shoulder, singing the lyrics. Many of the tunes had a wistful note, but they were also messages of hope.

Frieda played, "Coming In on a Wing and a Prayer," obviously an Air Force song. They sang the sentimental ones, too, such as, "It's Been a Long, Long Time" and the hopeful, "When the Lights Come on Again (All Over the World)." Everyone knew the tunes; across America they were frequently heard on radio. Even small children hummed and often voiced snatches of the lyrics.

"We must bring a bright and happy conclusion to the evening," Frieda announced. "This is a frequently played gay tune with lots of rhythm." She launched into, "Don't Sit Under the Apple Tree," making her fingers dance across the keyboard. Frieda sang with the others in loud, happy, singsong voices.

∼∾

Frieda was leaving the administration building after finishing her work for the day and there was Spider on the sidewalk near the building. Frieda noted to herself that they were still in a secure area. What did this mean for the Spider?

"Spider, I'm shocked to see you in Washington. It seems that you are many steps ahead of me. How do you get in and out of Germany with the war going on?" asked Frieda.

"Come, let's sit on a bench over in the park," said Spider.

They walked about a half a block to the nearest park bench, and Spider sat down beside her. He inquired about her job and how she liked it and whether she was satisfied with it.

"In a way, I feel that I am still helping Dirk, even though I don't know whether he is dead or alive," she responded. "At least, I am doing something to help defeat the German government and the chaos and war it has brought to so many of the European countries."

"Fraulein, I'm bringing you news of your Aunt Grace and Uncle Karl. First, they want you to know that they are safe at the present time. It was necessary for them to leave their home because of the heavy bombing in Munich. They are now in Schliersee with their daughter," explained the Spider.

"Yes," Frieda responded, "I have met my cousin. When we were her guests we had no idea that things would come to what they are now."

Spider continued, "Your Uncle Karl is practicing medicine in an effort to help the many refugees to the area around Schliersee. Your Aunt Grace assists him as a nurse. Together they make a good team. Your Aunt Grace now has a new purpose; she and your uncle are desperately needed."

"It's very thoughtful of you to bring the news of my family. Curiosity overcomes me though; did you come all the way to Washington for that reason? These are troublesome times and travel has to be very purposeful," Frieda noted.

"Fraulein, within the confusion of war, threads exist like a spider web of schemes that lead to a certain outcome," the Spider informed her.

Frieda responded, "I believe you're trying to tell me something that may affect my future."

"Yes, Fraulein, I'm going to make you an offer that will most certainly affect your future. I'd like you to give some thought to undertaking a new phase of work. Please meet with me tomorrow about the same time and same place. It's then that I will lay out plans for a possible new life," he said.

Frieda agreed to meet with the Spider the next day. In the meantime, she'd give some thought to what he had just said.

That evening Frieda slipped into her regular routine. She was faced with the same issues as when she had left Germany.

She was lonely and missed Dirk with all her heart. Her work in Washington was interesting and sometimes satisfying – and yes, sometimes even exciting; however, the war in Europe was still horrible and causing chaos and death, and she needed to think about a new future and whether she wanted something other than what she was doing now.

Coming face to face with this reality, Frieda acknowledged to herself that change might be good for her. Presently, she felt that she had reached a plateau in her work in Washington and it was becoming more and more a routine. Perhaps she could make an even more important contribution to the effort to defeat Germany and her allies in Europe.

The next day she once again approached a park bench where she would be meeting the Spider. This time, however, it was different than in Germany. In America, she was not afraid of being followed. She sat and waited for him; somehow it seemed that he was making sure there was no one else around to hear what they were saying.

They greeted one another and he sat down beside her and asked whether she was happy to be in the United States again.

"Yes, very. I don't have to worry whether or not I'm going to be arrested or that my uncle and aunt might be also."

The Spider chuckled and responded, "Well, my reason for being here may not be something you will be thrilled about in that case."

She sighed and said, "Please go on then, and tell me why we're here."

The Spider then presented a plan that could very well be a lifetime career for Frieda.

"I don't have to tell you that the war in Europe is still very much in full swing and the United States and Britain have their hands full with what is happening there and the very bloody war with Japan in the Pacific. I am afraid that the worst is still to come," the Spider said. "Your country needs all the help it can get to deal with a war covering a great part of the globe."

Spider continued, "The agency for which you work, the OSS, is heavily involved in work in Europe and they work with intelligence agencies of our allied countries as well as with underground groups in the occupied countries. They could use experienced people like you over there. Now that the European war seems to be moving into a decisive phase and the war with Japan doing the same, your country, and those of us who make our homes in Germany, need to begin to look to the future and what it may bring during the rest of this war and after it's all over."

Frieda was somewhat unsettled with all of this information and where it might be leading. Change would not come easy for her. She once again would have to resettle herself in an entirely new place. While she had long ago become independent of her mother and father, she always had a feeling in her heart that she would like to be near their comforting presence. But all of them now had their own lives and their own work to be done no matter what inner feelings they felt. What was it that Hans was going to propose?

Spider said, "Fraulein, I suggest that you take time to think about a commitment to working in Europe, doing what you can to help win this war. If you wish to continue working for the OSS organization, there is much you can do. Some of it would mean returning to Europe where your participation would be somewhat different than what you are doing here. You might even be loaned to British Intelligence so you could vary your experience and continue learning the intelligence trade. I suggest that you go home soon to your parents for a brief holiday and discuss this and your future with them. Think about whether you would be comfortable working in Europe at this stage of your life. We'll speak about this later. Now go home and get a good night's sleep and some well-deserved rest and relaxation."

A good night's sleep did wonders to clear Frieda's mind so she could contemplate over the weekend just what she should do. By Monday, she'd made up her mind to take up the offer of work in Europe, but she still had questions about it and wanted to get some of the answers as soon as she could. A week went by before she again encountered the Spider outside of her office. They walked slowly to the Park but didn't sit down. After a few pleasantries, the Spider paused and turned to Frieda, "Have you thought about what we have talked about?"

"I've been mulling it over almost all weekend and I'm not

fully rested. This is going to present a big change in my life. I miss Dirk and one of the things I am hoping will come out of my decision to accept your offer is that I will somehow be closer to him in Europe than I am here. Perhaps I may be able to trace his whereabouts somehow. At any rate, I'm willing to go. Will my work there be more dangerous than what I am doing here?" she asked.

"You'll be based in London, England, and working in the British Intelligence Service. The work done by the OSS in conjunction with British Intelligence in Europe, by necessity, has to be kept very secret. You would not be able to disclose who you work for or what you are doing. You will have a cover story to tell people who get inquisitive. I would use the same story with your parents. Any work done by the OSS and other like agencies can be dangerous.

"There are people among our enemies who don't like what we do and they may try and stop us. Depending upon what you want if you take this new job, I think that at some time or other you might be asked to be more active, perhaps even to the point of reentering Germany or one of the other occupied countries. Your ability to speak flawless German because of your parentage is why you are being given this chance to work in Europe. Of course, agreeing to more dangerous assignments would be entirely up to you, as there would be much more risk involved in an assignment like that. As you know, the Allied forces are bombing areas of Europe now. In other words, you would be in a war zone and subject to all that can befall someone there."

Frieda listened intently to the Spider with a feeling of apprehension — the same feeling she had when she and her fellow students were doing the pamphlets before the war escalated. Nevertheless, her feelings of helping to defeat the Nazis and, perhaps, finding Dirk again, were the stronger emotions and she said, "Hans, I am ready to go. All I need is to have a little time to close my affairs here and instructions on how to make the change."

He replied, "You can have at least a week for doing what you need to do. Your boss at the office and some of the other officers have already made contact with British Intelligence and they will help you with all the arrangements necessary to get you to London and take up your new assignments. I'll make some contacts with them and from there you will be in their hands for the change." The Spider lit a cigarette, took several pulls on it, and continued, "As for us meeting again, I'm sure we'll do so, but it will be somewhere in Europe. I'll let your Aunt and Uncle know what you are doing. I'm sure they will be concerned that you are doing this, but I'll do my best to keep their level of concern as low as possible."

Still Alive in Dachau

It was 1942, and Dirk was now beginning his second year at the Dachau Concentration Camp. As the war progressed, more and more individuals were being imprisoned at the camp, including Russians who had been captured during the invasion of the Soviet Union. Prisoners were now being assigned to work in some of the local industries nearby. Some were staying outside the camp so that they were available for longer work hours on site. Others were either marched or driven in trucks to their workstations where they stayed most of the time for 12 hours a day. Rations were not plentiful and, as the war was now in full swing, were continually reduced. Other prisoners, especially Jews, appeared to be worked to death as their rations were cut even more severely. Dirk was told that many died because of exposure to the elements, lack of food, exhaustion, sickness, and poor or no medical care.

One sector of the camp had now become notorious and it was told that prisoners who died were cremated in furnaces there. Large smoke stacks protruded above the lower profile of the camp buildings and belched smoke at various times. The extent of the deaths and reasons for the cremations were not always clear, but some of the prisoners had access to the area and knew for sure that Jews were being killed there and their bodies burned in the furnaces.

Dirk tried to keep a positive outlook and kept in mind that the war couldn't last forever and that one day he would be free and able to return to Frieda and his family. He had been able to write to his mother and father in Amsterdam, but he hadn't heard from Frieda; he had no idea where she was or what she was doing. Dirk's size, looks, and personality helped to keep him from trouble these two years. He avoided confrontations with the prisoners who held positions in the Labor Allocation Office where all the camp work assignments were made. His intelligence and education along with his connections helped him obtain a job in that office.

This identification disc was used by members of the Special Commandos who worked in the crematorium or elsewhere within the camp.

As time went on, and he was able to see all of the projects to which prisoners were assigned outside of the camp, he was able to arrange an assignment for himself outside of the camp. He went daily to Dachau to work in a paper factory located there. He worked in the office and coordinated where the daily influx of prisoner workers were to be assigned, kept track of them, and was responsible for seeing that they were fed while in the factory. He was respected and his record of staying out of trouble became known at the Labor Office and by the SS Führer in charge of it. His quarters remained in the Dachau Camp where he took his meals and slept.

In June 1942, Georg von Kessler, a Socialist prisoner running the Labor Office, stopped in at the paper factory where Dirk worked. Von Kessler was not often seen outside of the Dachau main camp. As he entered the office, he spotted Dirk's desk and headed directly over to it. "Hello, de Vries. Do you have a moment? I need to talk to you."

Dirk, surprised to see von Kessler, paused momentarily before replying, "Yes, by all means, sit down. I'm surprised to see you here."

Von Kessler dropped into a nearby chair and stretched his legs out saying, "Well, I periodically have to take a look around to see what the prisoner situations are in the factories or I'm in trouble with Sturmbannführer Kurlosik. He expects that we keep up our worker's production and will want to know the reason why if things don't look good for him. I don't want to end up being executed for sabotage of a war industry. With some of the major industrial areas being bombed time and time again, the government is depending heavily on production from dispersed factories in towns like Dachau. It was time for me to come here — and besides, I have something that might be of interest to you."

Dirk, with a grim look on his face, responded in a low voice, "Well, if they really wanted better production from us prisoners, they would feed us so that we would be able to work without getting exhausted. As it is, we are slowly starving and things appear to be getting worse. Don't they have any idea what better worker conditions would do for their war effort? Or are they as numb as I have always believed?"

Von Kessler snorted and said, "They aren't too much interested in whether you or I have plenty to eat. Prisoners are expendable and there are plenty of them. And besides, the armies fighting the Russians need to be fed. Things may get a lot worse before they get better, if they ever get better. But I didn't stop at your desk to bring you more food. As you may know, the SS has a porcelain factory in Allach and one here in Dachau. Not many prisoners work in them, but they are always looking for the right people to take on some of the jobs that would free up civilians working there for other jobs."

"Would you consider leaving your job here and going over to Allach to work there? It is SS-Reichsführer Himmler's pet project and produces some of the highest quality porcelain in Germany and, perhaps, anywhere in the world."

Dirk wondered why he was picked for this but suppressed

asking and replied, "Well, I'd like to know what I would be doing and if I have a choice, or are you just pushing me out of here to go there?"

Von Kessler responded, "No, I'm not pushing you anywhere. If you don't want to go, you don't have to, but you might find the work a little more interesting there. The head of the project is Obersturmbannführer Karl Diebitsch. He reports directly to the Reichsführer and you can expect Himmler and his crew to make appearances when they are in the area. I'm not sure exactly what they have in mind for you, but Diebitsch wanted someone who wasn't in the last stages of starvation and still had the ability to use his brain. You can think about it for a day or two and let me know. I wouldn't keep them waiting, though, if you want to go over there. They may change their minds."

Dirk thought about it for a day and before he went to work the next day he stopped in to see Von Kessler. "I'll give it a try. What do I do next?"

Von Kessler looked at him and said, "Well, report here in the morning, and I'll have a guard take you over to the Allach plant. The Obersturmbannführer wants to interview whomever we suggest for the job before he agrees to a change in work assignments."

Dirk did as he was told, and the next morning one of the SS guards took him to Allach. After a short wait in an outer office, he was admitted to the office of the factory director, Diebitsch.

"Sit down, please," Diebitsch said as Dirk entered the office. "We need someone to fill in behind one of our civilian employees who has been called up for military duty. You seem to have a decent work record at the paper factory and at the camp and have stayed out of trouble. So here you are to see if you fit what we want.

"I asked the Dachau Camp Arbeitseinsatzführer to send over someone who was in decent health and could use his brain. The work here is under the direction of Reichsführer Himmler's personal staff and he and they have a deep interest in what we do. Therefore, I don't think I need tell you that you will be expected not to make too many errors in what you do. Tell me a little about yourself, what you can do, and why you are having a forced vacation over at the Camp."

Dirk went over the circumstances of his job at the university in Munich and his subsequent arrest because of complaints about his attitude toward the Nazi regime. When he had finished, Diebitsch smiled and said, "Well, I'm sure that your attitude here will be more expansive as the assignment won't be as grueling as some I've heard about at the Camp. I don't think that you would want to go back to camp life and have to crack rocks 14 hours a day with a sledgehammer. The war will be over someday and they will probably want to quit feeding you and send you back to the Netherlands. At least I hope so."

"I think that you appear to be worth trying out, but I have to clear your work here with the Reichsführer. You'll be hearing more about this in due course, but, in the meantime, I suggest you ready yourself to make the change. We have a small barracks here where you will spend your time off the job. You will be on a detached assignment outside of the Dachau Camp itself and will not have to go back there unless we terminate your work here or for some other reason. You will not be free or able to circulate in the town and there are guards at the barracks."

Dirk continued working at the paper factory in Dachau. It was a week and a half later when von Kessler caught him returning from Dachau and told him that he was being transferred to the Allach factory and that the following Monday would be his first work day.

"A guard from the Allach plant will pick you and your things up sometime before the end of week. Good luck over there and remember to keep your mouth shut. Staying alive may depend on that."

Forty Years Later

Adrian just knew it; her friend would be the next person to walk through her office door. It was the first such incident that led her to believe that the two of them communicated on a higher level—like the time when her friend was in the hospital. Just before surgery, she had called Adrian's office to let her know. Adrian hurriedly answered the phone and her friend related where she was and why. Adrian said a quick prayer for her right there, standing at her desk. Later, her friend mentioned that she had actually seen Adrian's image as she prayed for her. It was floating before her.

The friend was old enough to be Adrian's mother. Adrian, however, was in the midst of a demanding job as well as responsibilities at home with a husband and teenage children. She knew her friend in the here and now. Adrian had to step back from her daily living patterns to even begin to understand that she didn't really know her at all.

Adrian respectfully addressed her friend as Mrs. de Vries. Although Adrian was a mature woman, she never in the world would've called the older woman Frieda. Mrs. de Vries had lived 60 years before meeting Adrian, and she did not speak freely of her life. As their relationship developed, however, she did give clues along the way.

Adrian became the privileged one, but didn't immediately catch on to that fact. Mrs. de Vries was a published writer rooted in academia. She had taught at several colleges and universities. Adrian had recently begun taking creative writing courses at the university several evenings a week, and she asked Mrs.

de Vries if she would be willing to critique some of her writings.

Mrs. de Vries replied, "Perhaps in my own time, my dear. I no longer make promises or keep deadlines."

Adrian realized that she had been very presumptuous to have asked for such a favor. She was undaunted, though, and counted on the fact that Mrs. de Vries would at some time be willing to read some samples of her work. And that she did, proving to be a tough critic. She did, however, note on one paper that it deserved an A rather than an A-, as marked by the instructor.

Their friendship grew in a cautionary way, given the fact that there were 20 years difference in their ages and experience. Mrs. de Vries invited her to the Women's Club to celebrate Adrian's birthday. Over dessert, the pianist began playing "Happy Birthday."

"Look across the room and acknowledge the pianist," Mrs. de Vries coached. At first Adrian had not realized that it was she who was being honored. This was the only time in her life that something so special had been done for her. It was a grand birthday celebration at Mrs. de Vries' club, the first of others to come. Adrian was to remember the coaching on that occasion as well as many other times throughout the years of their friendship.

Adrian gathered from first conversations that her mentor was from an upper-class family in Philadelphia. She had much to share with Adrian.

She concluded that Mrs. de Vries was an early example of a very liberated woman, one who was in certain ways not unlike women a generation or two later. Women were addressing various social issues of the time, and their campaigning brought these hornets' nests to the attention of the press, and consequently to local and national politicians. The suffrage movement affected more than one household and rattled many a husband as women campaigned for the right to vote. Mrs. de Vries had seen her mother absorbed with issues for liberation of women.

There came a time when Adrian no longer said, "That's just Mrs. de Vries. My, she's eccentric." Adrian came to wonder what life experiences had made Mrs. de Vries adapt to being alone, as well as strong enough to blaze a life of emancipation. What had caused her to be hostile, suspicious of authority figures, and cynical of Adrian's comment (he's a nice man) about an acquaintance?

Adrian was hurt and yet amused when Mrs. de Vries slammed the receiver in her ear one day during a phone conversation. The woman was filled with rage over something that had little importance in the overall scheme of things. Yes, Adrian had giggled softly and uncontrollably at something the other woman had said, and well deserved the rude bang in her ear.

Adrian knew Mrs. de Vries to be an adventurer who traveled solo around the world; one who sent postcards from Africa, India, Bali, and Japan. Photos from the South Pole showed her dressed in bulky outerwear for the climate. In another group photo, she was on a cruise ship dressed like a geisha, the theme for a Japanese event.

She boasted of going against the guide's caution in Africa while on a safari, putting herself in full view of tigers. She was a risk taker. Adrian wondered if Mrs. de Vries had lived through danger that made tigers somehow seem relatively safe. Mrs. de Vries' travel gifts might be raw silk from Japan or a turquoise-colored island dress from Bali.

"Oh, I've thought of ways to spend my money," Mrs. de Vries noted with glee. Her story of travels in India revealed shock over unsanitary conditions. It seemed that she ate candy for breakfast, lunch, and supper. Adrian regarded Mrs. de Vries' sweet tooth with pleasure; she had eaten candy rather than risk the local food. She was dismayed to see Indian women wipe down tables with water in which food had been cooked because there was no other available.

Mrs. de Vries wore exotic hats, showing her disdain for convention. A fur from Russia bore earflaps and a visor. Adrian admitted that the pull-down hat drew second glances as it graced the head of a woman who was about five-feet tall. Her clothing was atypical; she designed and crafted her dresses for the sake of expressing creativity and custom fit. And so the fabric belts grew longer and longer as the years went by. Her entire appearance was somewhat exotic—not following any particular style, but having a feeling of quality. The extravagant use of the finest fabrics purchased from countries around the world made her uniqueness very presentable.

Notes, letters, and gifts sparked Mrs. de Vries and Adrian's friendship. Adrian strung a necklace of semi-precious gemstones for her while she gifted Adrian with semi-precious jewelry from her own collection. Phone calls were infrequent and made when either of them chose to share something of importance. Mrs. de Vries' gifts of books were clues, not only to Mrs. de Vries' past, but to her life experiences as well.

A book about Quaker women in America hadn't held Adrian's attention until she reached for more clues to Mrs. de Vries' past. Quakers believe in equality of the sexes. Women coming from such families had never known anything else, and they were strong, independent women, able to stand on their own two feet. Historically, they had worked for the right of women to vote, as well as against social injustice in prisons and civil rights issues. They had encouraged the development of higher education and trained Quaker teachers.

Adrian was beginning to understand the profile of a woman like Mrs. de Vries. Her parents, as well as the ways of the Quakers, had made this strong independent woman whose roots were firmly planted in the liberation of women. Yes, her gender was superior or equal to men intellectually. Mrs. de Vries' life had been lived in a fight to empower women in what was essentially a man's world. At heart, after passing through a time in her life when love blossomed, she no longer accepted the male gender as superior in any way intellectually.

Included in the books Mrs.de Vries had given to Adrian was *Fireflies* by Rabindranath Tagore. The little poems were gems of thought that historically originated in the Orient. They were discovered written on fans and little pieces of silk. Adrian found them to be inspirational and deepened her desire to pen her own thoughts.

Searching through memorabilia, Adrian found a newspaper clipping, a feature story mentioning that Mrs. de Vries was a prolific professional writer. Her fiction, poetry, plays, and articles had been published in many national periodicals over a span of 20 years. A stage play written for children had particularly showed her interest for undertaking various literary forms.

A sense of mystery surrounded Mrs. de Vries. She spoke little of her past, and therefore one could only know her as she was in the present time. Adrian did perceive that there was disappointment and emptiness in her friend's life and maybe there was some bitterness as well. Perhaps it was something beyond bitterness; perhaps she detected her friend's angst in finding herself childless at a late age. Adrian remained in the dark as to when and what had happened to the husband, Mr. de Vries. Were memories so painful that she couldn't bear to speak of him or mention his name? Mrs. de Vries was unapproachable when it came to questions.

Mrs. de Vries Tells Her Story

"If you are going to write my story, you must be consistent in spelling my name correctly," Mrs. de Vries told Adrian one day. The married name is de Vries, with de being lowercase followed by a space. It is difficult to remember for Americans who are unfamiliar with the Dutch family names. We must spend more time together; I would like very much to tell you my story." And so she began a story of the bizarre events that had shaped her life.

"It was understood that I would go to Bryn Mawr after graduating from high school. Mother had ties with Bryn Mawr; in fact, she had graduated from there herself. I have had a lifelong connection with that school; Mother and I have given financial support to them over the years.

"After graduating from Bryn Mawr, for the sake of adventure and for furthering my education, I decided to go to Germany to earn a doctorate. Uncle Karl and Aunt Grace lived in Munich. They put out the welcome mat for me, and I looked forward to becoming better acquainted with father's brother and his wife. My parents were comfortable with my going to Germany, knowing that I would be in the care of family. Both of my parents had moved to the United States before I was born and so our little family was bilingual. I could speak fluent German in the same dialect of my parents who grew up in Koblenz.

"In America, there was little information about what was happening in Europe. After all, it was far from us geographically, and communication was hard to come by. England's Prime Minister, Winston Churchill, was doing his best to strike up feelings of sympathy for England. While Hitler was creating chaos in Europe, Churchill was making his point with President Roosevelt. This was taking place somewhat quietly since Americans felt very little need to become involved in a European war. Neither my parents nor I recognized impending political danger.

"I spent several months living in my aunt and uncle's home. It was a good way to get my feet on the ground while I began my studies at the university in Munich. After a time, I decided to strike out on my own and move closer to campus. It soon became evident that among the student population Munich was a hotbed of political strife.

"The person whose surname I bear, Dirk de Vries, was among other professors arrested on campus by the Gestapo, Germany's secret state police. Dirk and I had a love affair and my heart was broken. These events permanently changed my entire life.

"I chose to strike back at the Nazi regime. A group of students had organized a resistance effort to undermine National Socialism. The group of writers was modeled after the historical figure Mme. de Staël from the Napoleonic era. She too had a dramatic impact on my life. There are movements today that bear her name; these followers are writers mainly devoted to poetry. In this country, studies of her life and her work are included in the curriculum at certain universities. She has remained a woman of influence in the liberation of women.

"Our group of writers produced and distributed leaflets for the purpose of utilizing psychological warfare, particularly propaganda, to demoralize the Nazi war machine. Had we been caught and charged as enemies of the people, a death penalty could very well have been imposed.

"Adrian, it is best that these events be further enriched and detailed for the sake of a historical account. I have kept diaries of my life during this period of time. It is important for you to read my diaries and you will then be able to embellish my life story with detailed accuracy," Mrs. de Vries explained.

"Shortly after the war was over, word came from Aunt Grace and Uncle Karl. During the war, they had left Munich to go to their daughter's home in Schliersee. When they returned to Munich after the war, they found it to be badly damaged. Rubble was everywhere. Hunger was a primary concern. The days began with a search for food; the soup kitchens dispensed soup. Mandatory payment for a bowl of soup was a dead rat. This effectively helped rid neighborhoods of the vermin that had been unearthed and had multiplied."

Sophie Scholl

M rs. de Vries then told Adrian the story of Sophie Scholl. "Yes, there was more than one group organized for the purpose of conducting leaflet campaigns. One of them included a student named Sophie Scholl. Sophie Scholl, and the White Rose organization to which she and her brother Hans belonged, was operating parallel to my group. Sophie and her brother were Germans from a highly respected family. Sophie's brother was a leader in the Hitler youth organization; Sophie was a kindergarten teacher in the Labor Service of the Fatherland.

"Munich is the capital of the German state of Bavaria. It has been called the birthplace of National Socialism with its many links to Nazism. Munich also became a location for educated opposition to the Nazi regime. Students at the university were among those who joined in to try to counter the direction of Nazi regime.

"When Sophie arrived in Munich at the university, her brother, Hans, and a friend had already decided to mount an active resistance campaign against the Nazi regime. Sophie joined them in what became the White Rose, and it was said that Sophie was the heart and Hans, along with a friend, were the thinkers and planners. The leaflets produced by the group urged people to engage in passive resistance toward the Nazi regime.

"The White Rose produced at least six leaflets. Hans and Sophie distributed the sixth leaflet outside the lecture halls of the university and many in the school witnessed the act.

The incident was reported to a university administrator who reported it to the Gestapo.

"The high-speed trial for Sophie and Hans lasted less than three hours. The judge pronounced them guilty and the sentence was death by execution. Representatives of the Nazi state announced the sentence of high treason and aiding and abetting the enemy. Sophie was sentenced to death by guillotine. She and Hans died within a few seconds of one another."

More of Mrs. de Vries' Story

Mrs. de Vries continued, "Adrian, it is the story of a young German student who became a martyr in Germany. Although I am an American, our work in leaflet campaigns was the same. We did our work with leaflets before the war broke out or I would have never been able to leave Germany; I would have been interned. However, Sophie Scholl was one whose punishment was to be an example of what happens for engaging in treason against the regime during wartime. I was fortunate to have had an American passport making it possible for me to escape before I was apprehended.

"My life in Germany was marked by both good and bad experiences. I became well acquainted with my Uncle Karl and Aunt Grace. I loved and trusted them in the difficult times in which we found ourselves. They helped give a commonsense direction to my life.

"The darkest and ugliest was the arrest of the man I loved and admired above anyone I had met or could ever meet in the future. He is the one whose name I now bear; I carry all that he was close to my heart. He was a university professor accused of anti-Nazi activities. He had simply not supported National Socialism, and he along with other professors who shared his beliefs were arrested and taken to Dachau.

"A tragic history of Dachau prison camp has emerged since the war ended. For a while after his arrest, I carried the hope that he would somehow be found innocent of any charges against him, and he would be released. But this didn't happen, and he continued to be incarcerated. But he survived the camp, thank God. Part of my life since then and his imprisonment, was to study the history of Dachau prison camp; I plan to visit the historical remains of that camp sometime in the future.

"My education was aborted under the circumstances of political encroachment, the loss of academic freedom, and Dirk's arrest. I was studying to earn a Ph.D. in literature at the time, and I was thrust into mourning that absorbed me long after I returned home following my escape from Germany."

It was Adrian's time to ask questions. "Mrs. de Vries, tell me what your life was like in America after escaping Germany. I have an understanding of some of your life, but I'm sure there's so much more. As a writer, you were directed into the ways of academia. How did you use your writing abilities in a productive and lucrative way?"

Mrs. de Vries scanned past memories for successes that she might want to share with Adrian. "I was recruited to serve with the U.S. Army and the Office of Strategic Services in Washington, D.C., during the war. My training and education in writing served me well in the anti-Nazi leaflet campaign in Germany. The experience came to the attention of recruiters for the OSS. It did not require a great deal of training for me to pick up leafleting for the OSS in secret operations against Germany from America.

"Much of my adult life experiences have been recorded in diaries, with the exception of those years in Washington while I was working for the OSS. I do want to make these diaries available to you as you undertake writing my life story. However, everyone working for the OSS took oaths of secrecy. As far as the individuals go, we understood only our own involvement. Everything was orchestrated at a higher level of operations," she continued.

"The war was winding down. Those working in Washington planned a new future, making way for the government employees returning home from the war. I was offered a career position with the Central Intelligence Agency. The OSS was the forerunner of this new agency," Mrs. de Vries explained. "I stayed with them for a short time after the war but left for what I hoped would be a more constructive, fulfilling life and to make use of my education. Dirk had not yet reappeared and, needless to say, working for the CIA did not give me any opportunities to write and do the things that have filled my life since then.

"My dear Adrian, your birthday is coming up soon and I would like to invite you to have lunch at my place to celebrate. Yes, I can cook, as at times that was a necessity given the circumstances of where I lived. It's time for you to see my apartment and a wonderful view from a lofty height," Mrs. de Vries said with enthusiasm.

"I'd love to come. You're so special to me. I look forward to hearing where your life story next took you," Adrian responded.

～

Adrian rang the bell and entered the apartment where there was a magnificent view from the dining room. Mrs. de Vries had brought out her finest china, perhaps something that had come from her old family home in Philadelphia. Adrian actually wanted to turn a piece over and read the inscription on the back indicating where it was made and by what company. Her knowledge of antiques did not cover this particular pattern. She was curious but did not ask.

Lunch was well-prepared seafood, rice pilaf, and a salad. Of course, there was also dessert. Mrs. de Vries loved her sweets and so did Adrian. A cup of coffee, a candle-topped cupcake, and ice cream finished the birthday meal.

A beautifully wrapped package was on the sideboard and Mrs. de Vries handed it to her to open. A shimmering, full-length red silk robe cascaded from the wrapping paper. It was a gift only a mother would choose to give her daughter as a little indulgence. Tears came to Adrian's eyes with the realization.

"I'd like to share with you something more about my career and education, however, I don't believe that either of us have adequate time to give to this today," noted Mrs. de Vries."

Upon leaving the comfort and warmth of her company, Adrian thanked her profusely for the birthday celebration. Both knew that this was a one-of-a-kind day for them.

Mrs. de Vries embraced her, whispering, "I wish you were mine." They parted with tears of thankfulness that they had found one another.

~⌀

At another time, Adrian asked Mrs. de Vries if she had returned to Germany after the war.

"Yes, I was invited back by the de Staël League who awarded my doctor of letters degree from Munich University. Recognition for a collection of my writing became a part of the award. The de Staël League is a European writers' organization, one that had made a great difference in my life."

Adrian commented, "The doctor of letters degree helped to compensate for the fact that your studies were aborted in Germany because of the Nazi regime."

"Yes, it's surprising that some good things in Europe survived the war. Out of chaos, organizations such as the de Staël League were able to continue. They may have become broken and interrupted for a time; however, it is people who provide inspiration and a will for continuity," she remarked.

Mrs. de Vries continued, "The citation from the de Staël League validated my writing abilities, and in my own mind it became clear that my life's work was for a reason."

She proceeded to say that another connection to de Staël was a conference in 1988 at Rutgers University. It was the first international congress on de Staël in America. She had empowered generations of women and had become a model for anti-Nazi campaigns. The conference was devoted to the works of de Staël, the outspoken feminist of her time who was exiled from her native France by Napoleon. She had inspired women internationally, even women in the 21st century.

~⌀

Mrs. de Vries met with her travel agent to plan a trip to Germany. She made it clear that there would be two people traveling. It would be a guided bus tour that in part would allow them to walk the same paths she had traveled as a student during World War II.

The Berlin wall had been demolished November 9, 1989, and there was now some semblance of normalcy in Europe. It was a good time for her to return and also for Adrian to see places that had provided the setting for her friend's life as a student in Nazi Germany.

The two were well-matched travel companions. Adrian was convinced that her youth and energy would provide a safety net for Mrs. de Vries who was getting along in years. The trip would be an emotionally draining experience as well as physically challenging for Mrs. de Vries. She needed a friend.

Before the packing began, Adrian suggested to Mrs. de Vries that she might be more comfortable wearing trousers while traveling. This was something new for the older woman who had always dressed in skirts. After all, she had gone around the world with a reliable wardrobe that was based on wearing skirts. Adrian was convincing, however, and they eventually found outfits of tunics and trousers. At the first wearing, Mrs. de Vries now understood how Marlene Dietrich had influenced style for women. She was in love with the trousers and looked forward to a different kind of travel wardrobe.

"It must be a trip in the fall to take advantage of the pleasant weather and Oktoberfest in Munich. We have to have some fun, too," Mrs. de Vries said as she smiled.

As planned, in mid-September they began their trip, flying to Amsterdam where they joined a tour group. The bus driver was an Austrian who stayed with the group throughout their travels in Europe. A turnover of tour guides was evident; one in particular was Austrian.

There was to be a short stop in Cologne; however, it became somewhat longer when one of the travelers took off on her own to find a post office. It seems that she was so excited about being a world traveler that she showed her newness to group travel by adventuring on her own to find the post office.

Her travel companion went to find her and they both returned to the bus in half an hour. It was no surprise when the passengers showed their displeasure, chanting as the two walked the aisle of the bus; it seemed like a long mile.

Passengers who had been waiting on the bus took in the views around them. On the skyline the Cologne Cathedral rose high. Although far away, it was almost like an illusion. The impression was noteworthy, becoming a symbol that they would not soon forget.

Berlin had risen from what had been rubble. It was one of the most astounding things that postwar travelers could see.

Buildings rose mighty and strong, of stone and concrete, built in the ways of German architectural design and engineering. How remarkable it was. The program that helped to do all of this was the Marshall Plan and it was the American taxpayer who had helped pay for it.

The bus traveled a highway along the Berlin wall. The wall stretched more than 103 miles and was 10-feet high. From a tourist point of view the colorful graffiti was a distraction from its painful history. Sections of the wall were still standing; however, much had come down.

The watchtowers, mines, trenches, and alarms had long been dismantled. The dogs, guards and their machine guns were only history. The day the wall came tumbling down, masses of humanity poured across what had once been an immovable border.

"We're approaching Checkpoint Charlie. Feel free to leave the bus and take a break," the tour guide announced.

Adrian commented as they left the bus, "I don't believe this is meant to be a bathroom stop."

Mrs. de Vries noted that there were no obvious facilities that would accommodate the busload of passengers.

Americans had heard the often-used phrase Checkpoint Charlie. It had been frequently repeated in the Cold War news; Adrian and Mrs. de Vries were passing through the famed checkpoint.

The tour guide explained that Checkpoint Charlie was designated as a crossing point for foreigners and members of the Allied forces. East Germans referred officially to Checkpoint Charlie as the border crossing point. The Berlin wall was erected by the East German government in 1961. A year later, an East German teenager was shot by East German guards while trying to escape to the West.

They boarded the bus and Mrs. de Vries looked at their itinerary saying, "We're going to the eastern sector for an overnight stay at a resort on a lake there. I believe it was a retreat for German military officers for rest and relaxation during the war."

As the bus headed into the eastern sector, Adrian commented with candor, "It should be interesting. The road ahead is narrow and nothing but dirt. Look at the ruts."

The tourists were too naïve to be frightened. Adrian admitted some unease when the tour guide walked up front to consult with the driver, and there she stayed. Both she and the driver continued their discussion, appearing to be somewhat anxious.

Borders had been opened too recently to allow for mapping of the eastern sector; the bus was traveling a roadway that was not meant for a tour bus. The road was rugged. Rain would have made it impossible to travel and there was no map.

The bus lurched around a curve in the road. It was an anxious moment as passengers found they were facing an ancient stone dwelling. The structure was only a few yards from the roadway. Nearby was an equally ancient-looking beast of burden. The oxen stood next to its wooden cart at the side of the house. It was breathtaking, not only for the element of surprise, but for its rugged beauty as well.

Turning left, the bus followed an even narrower lane. It was also a heavily rutted dirt path leading to the resort, the destination for that night. Darkness had fallen and the lighting around the buildings was very dim.

The travelers found even the lobby of the hotel to be poorly lit; dinner was adequate but certainly not sumptuous. They had few expectations at this point other than the fact that it was interesting to see the postwar eastern sector. Political changes and reorganization had not yet offered time or resources to modernize. Adrian and Mrs. de Vries climbed a flight of stairs to their adjoining rooms. They were indeed weary travelers.

After breakfast the next morning, they walked out on a plaza overlooking a beautiful lake. The sun was not shining and through the dampness and chill, Adrian and Mrs. de Vries were still able to appreciate the outstanding location of the resort.

Back on a highway again, there was even greater evidence of the political changes that were taking place. Mrs. de Vries was following the itinerary.

"It's unsettling. The itinerary indicates that we are backtracking on the same path that we had taken earlier. This town had a different name when we last traveled through," Mrs. de Vries remarked.

Adrian exclaimed, "Look, they're pulling down that huge statue in the center of town! It must be a political figure from the old regime."

Looking across the aisle at a fellow traveler, Adrian heard him say to his wife while laying a hand on his stomach, "Put out the fire, just put out the fire."

The gentleman had apparently been overindulging in German food and beer.

～

The tour bus pulled into a parking lot for tourists who wished to see the Eagle's Nest. Adrian and Mrs. de Vries, along with others, boarded a smaller bus to travel the 2,600-foot mountain. Only 13-feet wide, the road was built for a single lane of traffic; drivers were equipped with radios to keep traffic flowing. The road was steep and the going slow.

The Eagle's Nest was commissioned as a 50th birthday present for Hitler on April 20, 1939. Hitler had little association with the property, visiting about 10 times for half-hour visits. Because of his apparent disassociation, the property was saved from demolition after the war. Dwight D. Eisenhower, supreme commander of the Allied forces in Europe and later President of the United States, wrote that the U.S. Army's Third Infantry division was the first to seize the Eagle's nest.

A large elevator took the tourists the last 407 feet up to the Eagle's Nest. The elevator was finished with polished brass, Venetian mirrors, and green leather. It opened to the main reception room where a fireplace of red, Italian marble was the first feature to catch the eye. A gift from Mussolini, it had been damaged by Allied soldiers who removed chips for souvenirs. The wedding reception for the sister of Eva Braun had been held here in 1944. Eva Braun was Hitler's mistress.

Mrs. de Vries and Adrian went through the double doors to the outside. They followed a path climbing to a higher level. From the peak they had a magnificent view of the Alps, a view that most certainly had to be captured.

Adrian said, "We must take pictures of this view. I have a camera for panoramic shots. It's a disposable one that I brought just for making this trip. It's easier to manage while going through airport security."

Mrs. de Vries said, "Yes, I agree. Airport security sometimes holds people up. We certainly wouldn't want that to happen when we're with a tour group; it would mean that the whole busload of people must wait for clearance. I've heard of that happening when one in the party held up everyone while waiting for security to take apart her camcorder."

She continued, "I do hope that you will have an extra set of photo prints made for me when we get home again."

They returned to the reception area and to the elevator. Their visit to the Eagle's Nest had been between mealtimes; there was no evidence of food being served in the dining room.

Oktoberfest in Munich

"What in the world is planned for us at Oktoberfest? Our events confirmation shows that we're to have stand-up seats," Adrian commented excitedly.

Mrs. de Vries replied, "I'm not sure I like the sound of 'stand-up seats.' It certainly implies that we'll stand more than sit during the parade."

Both agreed that whatever was in store for them would be a new adventure.

At the parade, Adrian felt that she had walked into a theater to see a performance in Technicolor. Their seats were indeed stand-up. However, their space had been reserved for them. They could actually hold on to the ropes that separated the crowd from the parade.

Families in colorful Bavarian costume passed before their eyes, along with riflemen and historic coaches and performers. The handsome teams of horses were proud and wonderful as they pulled the coaches and beer wagons.

The marching band was approaching them when one member caught Adrian's eye. He began a hurrah that swept through the entire platoon. Both Mrs. de Vries and Adrian were flattered—in fact, they were exuberant. It had become an interactive parade.

The sounds of traditional German music drew them to the beer tent. Adrian and Mrs. de Vries entered into the excitement as they watched the dancing and the brass bands playing "oom pah pah" music. Everyone knew the words; they sang, swaying and standing on the benches as the liter tankards had their effect.

Seated at a picnic-style table, Mrs. de Vries and Adrian ordered beer. The server soon arrived carrying a fistful of liter mugs in each hand.

Mrs. de Vries commented, "Watching them carry the heavy tankards, I can only think of the arthritis that most certainly will strike them later in life."

There is drama in holding a liter mug, something that neither of them had done before. Mrs. de Vries supported the mug with both hands; it was predictable that they were unable to drain the heavy glass tankards.

Only in Munich at Oktoberfest would this be an acceptable, spontaneous gesture. Sitting at the table nearby, a group of Italians were enjoying the festival. One young man approached their table, giving them each a kiss on the cheek. In the gaiety of the moment, this was a wonderful, generous thing to do. The festival was indeed a meeting place for people of many countries.

Later that evening at the hotel, Adrian found a brochure that Mrs. de Vries had wanted. She went next door to her room and knocked lightly on the door. She tried again and there was still no response. Thinking that Mrs. de Vries had gone to sleep early, Adrian returned to her room, forgetting to mention this to her later.

～

A chill passed through her body. Mrs. de Vries felt in a state of shock with the thought of Dachau. She said to Adrian, "My dear, I don't think I can do this. I can't bear to put myself in this place to trace the footsteps of my Dirk. I won't be able to stand seeing and hearing about what the prisoners had to go through."

Mrs. de Vries continued, "I had a recurring dream last night. Dirk was standing at the foot of my bed. He was trying to tell me something; however, I was unable to understand him. The dream was too real. It became lifelike, and I am unable to forget the experience."

Mrs. de Vries continued, "One thing that makes this visit bearable is anger. Yes, I have been angry for many years over the arrest of Dirk. I'm also angry for the suffering and death that Hitler caused many human beings. Most recently, however, I'm angry with our Austrian tour guide who speaks of Hitler's good points. It is totally out of balance. The evil was monstrous."

As the bus approached the entrance to Dachau Concentration Camp, a new tour guide from the camp itself took over.

Trees lined the perimeter of the camp outside a wire fence. It was evident that the trees lacked vigor. The young guide told a story that one could not forget: a story that could become legendary.

Simply stated, she said, "The birds have never returned."

Nature itself — the birds and animals, the grass, trees, and the air — had been stricken by the sights, sounds, and stenches of the inhumanity that had taken place here. Nature remembered the smell and feeling of death, and the memory did not go away.

Her anger was as cold and hard as steel. It did, however, serve the purpose of killing the emotions. Mrs. de Vries set one foot ahead of the other and with purpose she looked at the site where Dirk had been taken along with thousands of other prisoners. The population reached its peak in 1944 when it held 60,000 prisoners.

The total number of inmates fluctuated because of incoming and outgoing transports and the systematic policy of extermination in the camp. At the time of liberation, about 32,000 prisoners were left. Every day, about 200 prisoners died of starvation and typhus. A diet of about half the normal calories ended up reducing people through starvation and hard work.

During the war, the population was made up of Poles, Russians, French, Yugoslavs, Germans, Jews, and Czechs. A number of other national groups — Belgians, Hungarians, Italians, Austrian, and Greeks — were among them in fewer numbers.

The prisoners were divided according to the type of crime for which they had been found guilty — political prisoners and criminal prisoners. Dachau was set up in 1933 and was liberated by the Allies in 1945.

The Americans came on Sunday, April 29, 1945. A Jeep arrived. The first American was hoisted into the air. Two others, a 19-year-old farmer from the West and a 19-year-old university student, were dragged out of the Jeep and carried around the grounds on the shoulders of the newly freed prisoners.

Adrian and Mrs. de Vries walked away from the small museum and informational building where they had sat on benches while watching films of Dachau. They had feelings of oppression. There was no escape from what they had just learned.

Adrian and Mrs. de Vries walked a short distance to the toilet facilities. By now, both of them were spooked. Doors to the individual toilets were made of heavy steel and very high; they closed efficiently like trap doors. Adrian wondered if she would ever be able to get out and told herself not to panic. Locks on bathroom stalls had always made her uneasy; however, this was not an ordinary door.

Continuing their tour, they saw a gate leading outside of the camp. It was a wide arched gate bearing the words, "Work Sets You Free."

Mrs. de Vries' emotions broke through upon seeing a brick oven. It was freestanding in the open field, the remainder of the larger crematorium that had once been housed under a roof with walls.

Adrian put an arm around Mrs. de Vries' shoulders and steered her in the direction of the tour bus. She did not want the broken woman to see the large sculpture representing life-size emaciated bodies and skeletons stacked upon one another. The outdoor sculpture was configured in weathered black steel.

Dachau had been a sobering experience for the tour group. Silence was pervasive during the bus ride back to the hotel. The tour guide, not wishing to make this day altogether sad, suggested that they all return to their rooms and freshen up. She invited them to be her guests for a round of drinks in front of the hotel fireplace before dinner.

Return from Europe

Upon returning back home from Europe, it was time for Mrs. de Vries to take some quiet restful time. Soon she regained her old enthusiasm and energy, and she called Adrian to see if the photos were back from the photo shop.

Adrian said, "I just picked them up yesterday. For the most part they have turned out well. It's so exciting to see them and remember the places we visited. The panoramic shots are spectacular."

They arranged a meeting to go over the photos and reminisce. Adrian tried to understand what Mrs. de Vries was feeling about the country that had caused her so much pain.

"The Germans who are liberal minded want people outside of Germany to know they are no longer Nazis. They want to bury the past," concluded Mrs. de Vries.

She continued to say that she was not yet ready to let it be buried too deeply. Her writings often included a longing for lost friends and hinted of painful memories. They continued to express sorrow for all of the college professors who set forth initiatives for academic freedom. "Adrian, I have devoted my life to enlightenment and freedom of expression. I have done this to honor those who lost their lives because of what took place in Europe during the Second World War. I can never forget what happened."

"Now that we are home, I no longer see or feel your anger," Adrian observed.

"Anger is not a good thing to carry in one's life. I have to admit that I've dipped in and out of it at various times. My very best writing has come when I am at peace, when I am able to experience a higher energy beyond myself. This is where I find inspiration.

"There is something I would like to share with you," Mrs. de Vries said. "At the time of our recent visit in Munich, I met with Hans the Spider one evening. I've been in touch with him for many years. He has come to me at various times when I have had problems or serious decisions to make. It seems that in some cases he has crossed the ocean for me. He lives in Munich, making it a good time for me to see him again.

"As you remember, I credit the Spider for having made arrangements for me to leave Germany when the Nazis were on my heels. The people whose lives he saved, he does not forget. He takes a special responsibility for their welfare. I am one of those," Mrs. de Vries confided.

She continued to say that he had grieved with her at the death of Aunt Grace and Uncle Karl. After all, he had been their neighbor. He first became aware of her as their niece when she lived with them for several months.

Adrian asked, "Do you have any idea what his personal life has been like?"

Mrs. de Vries shared little, "He and I have had much in common, although we have been separated by thousands of miles. To my knowledge he never married. He was involved with the anti-Nazi underground at a time when most young men would have otherwise been thinking of marriage."

What came next, Adrian found very exciting. It was a part of Mrs. de Vries' life story that she had never before mentioned – a story of events that had led to further intrigue.

"Adrian, I'm going to tell you some things about my life that I've never told anyone else. I trust you since you have been one of my faithful friends and we've shared some moments together that I think we both enjoyed. You already know most of my story, but there is some of it I haven't disclosed because I worried that I shouldn't say anything about it. I'm going to tell you the rest of the story that took place after I was recruited for the OSS in Europe. The OSS doesn't even exist anymore, so I doubt there is anything that hasn't been made public about its activities. And certainly, the incidents in which I participated have all been published in one way or another in some of the post-war history books."

Mrs. de Vries began her story. "It all really began with my work in Washington with the U.S. Army and my decision to move to London and continue the work in Europe. This is the part of the story that you don't have any knowledge about. I was offered a position with the OSS in London, and after dallying around for several weeks, trying to make up my mind, I accepted the assignment. I thought my efforts might contribute in some way to the shortening of the war over there. It also might have led to clues of the whereabouts of my professor if he was still alive.

"My arrival in England was during winter when the weather there is not pleasant. Cold, clammy, cloudy, and rainy can sum up the day I arrived in London. I was not in the best of moods anyway, as I was apprehensive about what I had decided to do. I was met at the railway station in London by a young, smiling, English woman named Fiona Davis."

Dirk at the Allach Porcelain Factory

Dirk remained one of the lucky ones who was caught in the web of the Gestapo and Germany's concentration camp system. He was working outside of the Dachau Konzentrationlager and, while still a prisoner and under guard during his off duty time, was in a work environment that was not aimed at wearing down the worker and pushing him to eventual sickness and possible death from an inadequate diet and exposure to the elements. He had worked a number of months now at the factory and had gained trust and respect for his work from the SS personnel and civilians assigned to the factory and business.

Dirk's work had varied and he had done manual labor in the factory as well as more specialized work necessary in the manufacturing process of the porcelain pieces being produced. Many of these were quite historical in nature. Others were pieces that glorified German culture and the various facets of the National Socialist ideals. All were exquisitely designed and intricate in their individuality. Many were given by Himmler to various supporters or heroes of the Reich and as Dirk had been warned, Himmler made several stops at the factory when he was nearby. His visits and presence were usually presaged by much scurrying about and assuring that the factory and offices were relatively spotless.

Recently, Dirk had been working with factory personnel who were securing the various clays and minerals used in making the porcelain. He had learned about kaolinite, feldspar, and other minerals such as alabaster and soapstone used in its manufacture. The factory was always on the lookout for sources of these different minerals and especially those with properties that might increase the quality of the porcelain produced by the factory. Dirk was working in the mineral warehouse one day when Hauptsturmführer Radtke approached him. Radtke and most of the other SS personnel assigned to the Allach project were members of the Allgemeine SS, the branch that ran much of the business and administrative functions of Reichsführer SS, Himmler's massive organization.

The Allgemeine (or general) SS had no police or military duties usually and personnel were somewhat easier to deal with than with the Totenkopf or Death's Head formations who were the concentration camp overseers. Wilhelm Radtke was assigned to the procurement of materials for the production of the porcelain. Radtke had been an accountant with a Düsseldorf newspaper in his civilian life before the war.

"Herr Professor, how would you like to take a trip with me to investigate a supply of kaolinite and other materials in the Ukraine?" he said as he stopped next to Dirk. "Oberstumbannführer Diebitsch has some information about a source of kaolin in the Ukraine and wants someone to go out there and see if it is something we can use here. If it is, I'm to set up some arrangements for procurement and bring some of it back here for making a few test pieces. I can use your help with handling and getting the materials separated and ready for application here when we get back. It will be a small wartime vacation."

Radtke was Dirk's immediate supervisor and so Dirk had little doubt about where he would be headed in the next few weeks. "Well, Herr Radtke; as you know, I am totally committed to your service, and as always am ready to do your bidding. All I need to know is when you plan to leave, and I'll get things in order here for leaving. You do know that there is a war going on and how close do we need to get to that?"

Radtke laughed and said, "Don't worry your head about that. I've not got any plans to get anywhere near where the lead is flying. In fact, this location we have to look at is in the western part of the Ukraine. The Ukrainians have welcomed us there and many of them are working for us. I think that the area is pretty secure and we should be able to have a picnic as well as take care of our other jobs. This is a part of our new German territory that we'll settle when we get the front stabilized and the Russians beat. You can begin getting your things together, and we'll probably leave sometime next week. I'll let you know more a little later when I get things arranged. We'll have a couple of guards along to keep us company."

Dirk nodded. "I'll be ready to go whenever you say."

A week later Dirk found himself and Hauptsturmführer Radtke along with three very tough-looking non-commissioned officers from the Totenkopf unit at Dachau, boarding a JU-52 tri-motored Luftwaffe plane to fly to the city of Lvov in the Western Ukraine. Dirk was taken aback when he saw the three guards and what they were bringing along. All three of them appeared to be armed to the teeth — even to the extent of having machine pistols among their gear. During a moment when they were alone, Dirk turned to Radtke and said, "It does appear as though we are going to go to war from the looks of our companions on this trip. I thought I heard you say that we wouldn't be near any flying lead."

Radtke glanced at the three guards loading their gear into the aircraft and then at Dirk. With a grimace he said, "That wasn't my idea. Obersturmbannführer Diebitsch wanted to be sure that nothing happened to us since we would be in rural areas outside of Lvov. He wanted to make sure that we get back to the factory without problems from bandits or locals. I doubt that we will need any of their hardware so don't worry about it."

Dirk wasn't at all satisfied by Radtke's response, but there was nothing he could do about the situation. The two men moved to the aircraft stairway and boarded the plane. As soon as they were seated, the JU-52 taxied to the end of the runway and took off. They were on their way to Lvov.

JU-52 (Courtesy of Bundesarchiv-Federal German Archives)

Working for the Brits

Frieda got into the car, and Fiona greeted her gaily and pulled away from the station. She introduced herself to Frieda and said, "I'm going to be a sort of companion or a shadow to you for a while until you get your feet on the ground. The people here want to make you as comfortable as possible. So if you have any questions or needs now or after you get settled, please let me know. I will be living in rooms very near to yours in the same building, so it should be easy for you to get in touch if you need to do so. How was your trip across the pond? I've heard it isn't exactly a pleasure these days."

Frieda liked Fiona's easy manner and answered, "Well, it got quite rough several times coming over and once there was an alarm. Someone thought they saw the periscope of a submarine so we had to worry about that for a while. And to top that off, I got quite ill several times when the boat was rocking so badly. But I made it and am very glad to get off the ship. I'm quite interested in who I'll be working with and what I'll be doing here. How long have you worked for this organization and are you able to say what you do?"

Fiona glanced over and replied, "It's been two years now since I began work here. I joined the group just after we declared war on Germany. I wanted to do my part. We've had a number of refugees come over and what they say about things in Germany and the occupied countries is not very good. The Nazis can be very nasty when they want to be, and they are not treating the Jews very well, but I'm sure you have heard about that already. As for what I do, I will be working in the same section in which you are. We will be translating various pieces of intelligence that we obtain and writing summaries for our blokes to do something with. Some of our work will be to translate material found in newspapers from Sweden and Switzerland. They aren't at war with Germany and so things are reported that help us determine how the morale is in Germany and other little things we wouldn't otherwise hear about. I understand that you are very fluent in German and that must be the reason that they've set you up to start in our department."

As she finished speaking, she pulled up to a gate at which an armed guard stood and stopped. A sergeant of the British Military Police came over to the window and said, "Hello, Fiona," and asked for her identification. After a quick look, he opened the gate and they drove into a large compound. The compound appeared to be a large estate. There was one very large mansion and several smaller buildings set around the rather spacious acreage. Fiona drove up to the entrance to one of the smaller buildings and stopped the car.

"Well, here is our home away from home. I'll help you with your luggage," Fiona said as she took hold of one of Frieda's large suitcases. The two women entered the building, which had been renovated somewhat to serve as living quarters for females. Fiona showed Frieda her own rooms on their way to Frieda's, which were just a few doors down the hall. Frieda had four rooms in the small apartment; it was fully furnished and looked quite cozy.

After dropping Frieda's suitcase, Fiona moved to the door and said, "Well I'll leave you to recuperate from the trip. I'm sure it must be wonderful not to have the floor moving up and down. There's a tele over there and you can contact me by just giving the operator my name. We have a dining hall in the building just to the left as you go out the door to the drive. If you are hungry tonight, give me a call on the phone and I'll go over with you for a bite. If not, I'll be over in the morning at 0700 hours so we can go for breakfast, and then we'll meet the people with whom you will be working."

Frieda thanked her and told her that she would see how she felt later. Then she proceeded to unpack and make herself comfortable. So far she liked what she saw. They were evidently on the edge of London, and it did not look like bombing had come anywhere near the compound as yet. The rooms were cheerful, clean, and adequate, although not spacious. Besides the toilet and small kitchen, there was a bedroom and a living room. After she had unpacked her clothes and put them away, she stretched out on the bed and almost instantly fell asleep. The trip had exhausted her. When she awakened, it was almost midnight, and after she had made herself ready for bed and set the alarm, she crawled back into bed and fell into a deep sleep.

Promptly at 0700 the next morning, Fiona rapped on the door and greeted Frieda when she opened it. They walked to the dining hall cafeteria and went through the serving line for their breakfast. As Fiona sat down, she said, "Well, eat a good breakfast, Frieda. You will need it, as it will be a busy day. After we eat, we'll be going to the office of Major Albert McConnell and he will be the person with whom you can discuss your job. He is going to want to know everything about you.

"Since you're a civilian employee, you won't be subject to military routines and discipline, but be aware of it and give it its due. There is a war on and England is fighting for its life. The military wants things to run like clockwork," Fiona continued.

Major McConnell's office was on the third floor of the mansion. The British Government had either commandeered the property or purchased it. Its location in an area of the spacious estates that surrounded it assured that it could not be easily identified as a possible bombing target. Frieda was nervous as she entered Major McConnell's office.

The major was a middle-aged man with sandy hair and a mustache. He looked up and smiled at Frieda, saying, "Welcome to England, Ms. de Vries. I hope that Fiona has made you comfortable and told you a few of the things you need to know about this place."

Frieda replied, "Yes, she has been very helpful, and I'm glad to have someone I can get help from if I need it. I'm excited to learn more about what I will be doing here. I was in Germany and barely got out just ahead of the Gestapo. I've had some experience with what is happening there. My fiancé was arrested and sent to Dachau Concentration Camp, even though he is a Dutch citizen. I've had no contact with him since he was sent there, and prior to leaving Germany, was not able to get any information about him from the police."

The major frowned as he lit his pipe. "I'm sorry to hear about your troubles. Perhaps you will be able to reunite with him after this damn war is over. A lot of people in Europe are finding themselves in German concentration camps these days, so he isn't alone.

"As you may know, we are looking for people to help us compile information and intelligence about the enemy. You were recommended to us because of your language ability. We're grateful to your country for the help we have gotten from it and for loaning you to us for a period of time. You'll be working on the second floor of the building in which you ate breakfast. Fiona is one of the people who will work with you. Your major task to begin with will be to familiarize yourself with what we do in Section 4 and what the details of your work will be. Captain Lawrence is in charge of the section and will be your immediate supervisor." Major McConnell proceeded to ask Frieda about her work history with the U.S. military and OSS and more about her experiences in Germany while she was at the university.

The discussion lasted more than an hour and when Frieda was finished, the major thanked her and sent her to the building that would be her place of work for a while in England. She reported to Captain Lawrence. He was a much younger and very good-looking man, who sat in a glassed-in office in one corner of a large floor space. The space accommodated at least a dozen desks. Frieda spotted Fiona right away and waved to her as Captain Lawrence escorted her to a desk a little distance from Fiona's. The captain pulled up an adjacent chair and they began discussing the various aspects of her new job.

"I'd like you to talk to Lieutenant Griffin in the morning. He's our orientation specialist. He will go over the chain of command, what we do here, and how your job fits in to it all. He'll also explain what we want you to pull from some of the material you will review, how to compile reports, and other aspects of the job."

Frieda listened intently to what she was being told and left the office when the Captain finished.

She reported for work the next morning, and as she was

sitting down at her desk, Lieutenant Griffin walked up. He greeted her and asked her to follow him to another office on the same floor. After introducing himself and finding out some things about Frieda, he began orienting her more specifically to the work they were doing. This went on for most of the morning. After she and Fiona had eaten lunch, she returned to the Lieutenant's office.

"I hope we didn't cover everything too fast this morning. If you have questions or need to discuss something, you can talk either to the captain or me. Now, I'd like to discuss your assignment. We'll start you off with going through German newspapers sent to us from abroad or transcripts of radio broadcasts. You'll need to review each for any kind of clues as to how they think the war is going, what is happening in Germany, and the morale of the people. Look for the effects of our bombing, what shortages there are, and some of the other things we covered during the orientation. At the end of each day, you will use your writing skills to draft up a report on what newspapers you have reviewed and your findings about the situation in Germany. This report you will submit to my secretary, and that will end your day."

And a new phase of Frieda's work began where she was on loan to the British intelligence service. For a month, she carried out her daily assignment of reading German newspapers and reporting what she had found. Having lived in Germany for several years, Frieda was provided with an insider's view of the situation and how the country might be affected by the war. Her association with her uncle and aunt, who had a major stake in Germany's future, along with her involvement at the university, resulted in a realistic insight with which to tackle her work. Her reports were detailed, well written, and gave a thoughtful and relevant view of what might be occurring in Germany.

After several months, Lieutenant Griffin called her in on a Thursday and told her she was being given a new assignment. "Frieda, we'd like you to go on a detail from this office and sit in on prisoner interrogations we're starting at several British prisoner-of-war camps. We want you to provide us with an accurate translation of what they say. We have selected several prisoner-of-war camps north of here for this program, and I am going to send you to one in Scotland."

Frieda on Loan to British Intelligence

"A facet of your work with the prisoners will be to look for intelligence that will help us provide more accurate information about the morale and situation found in the German armed services and their homeland. The prisoners at the camp are ardent Nazis or have served in the SS. A few of them are from the Belgian, French, and Norwegian SS units. We are hoping that the presence of a woman interrogator will lower the prisoner's guard and they will be willing to talk more freely than if interrogated by male intelligence officers. I'll provide you with a schedule of reporting before you leave and the information you compile will be brought here for further processing. I've arranged for you to leave on Monday. Tomorrow, please pick up railway tickets for Glasgow at our service desk. Captain Grant Smythe will be the man to whom you report during your stay at the camp."

Frieda left the following Monday for Scotland. She relaxed as she traveled through the countryside of England and Scotland and soaked in the green and lush rural scenery. The rolling hills and the picturesque villages through which they passed were untouched by war. Her thoughts wandered from her parents and home in the United States to thinking about Dirk and wondering if he were still alive. Her thoughts returned to the many wonderful times they had attending art and musical events and the intimate moments of their love.

No one had heard from Dirk since the letter from Josef

revealed that he was at the Dachau Camp and working in a factory in the town. She was saddened by the thoughts of what could have been had there been no war. How could there be such men who would deliberately set out to wage war against people who were peacefully trying to live out their lives. When she thought of the events at the university in Munich, bitter feelings flooded like acid over her mind. The landscape slowly changed as her train made its way to Carlisle and then toward Glasgow. She was lost in her thoughts.

An army sergeant met her at the terminal, introduced himself, and escorted her to a dun-colored Ford parked outside. They immediately headed east toward the prisoner-of-war camp, which was near a town called Milton Bridge some 50 miles from Glasgow.

"Have they told you much about Woodhouselee Camp, Miss de Fries?" the sergeant asked as they drove through the countryside and the gathering darkness.

Frieda responded, "Very little. I was told you have some fanatical Nazis there, and I'm a bit frightened at the thought of being in the presence of a group of men who might try anything to get back to Germany."

The sergeant chuckled and said, "Yes, there are some real blighters there, but I think for most of them, they are a little glad they are out of the front lines for the duration of the war. But the officers are another thing. And they very well could organize escapes and force or encourage some of their subordinates to take part in it. But let's not worry about that. The British Army is there to protect you and we bloody well will do it."

They arrived in the evening after darkness had fallen; the sergeant took her directly to several buildings that housed officers and female employees. A duty officer signed her in and showed her the quarters she would call home for the next three or four months. It was a barren set of rooms with a toilet. She would have to take her meals at a nearby officer's mess hall, which was equally barren. There were several other women who worked at the camp and they, too, would be served at the mess hall.

The next morning, Captain Smythe knocked at her door and introduced himself. "Welcome to Scotland and our little prison camp in the hills, Ms. de Vries. I thought it would be friendly to pick you up and take you to breakfast before we do any serious talking about your work here. I understand you are a little nervous about your being here, but I think that after you are here a while and enjoy the camp food for a few days, all thoughts of life elsewhere will pass away," he laughed sarcastically.

Frieda smiled and said, "Captain, I'm going to try and be ready for everything. I signed up in hopes I could do something to help end the war; for now, I'll just put my shoulder to the wheel and do my best."

Following breakfast, they left the mess hall and strolled over near the main gate of the camp. "Behind all this wire and those watchtowers, we have some of the tough nuts of National Socialism. Those Quonset huts house a lot of people captured during some of our raids along the coast of France and in other places. And some of them are not happy about being behind this wire," Captain Smythe told Frieda. "They are relatively harmless now and most see the necessity of cooperating with us."

After a short walk along the wire and looking into the camp, they walked to Captain Smythe's office and he proceeded to orient her to what she should expect. "Most of these men who appear to be someone who might have more information for us or hiding their identity will be sent to London for further interrogation. We will tag them as persons of interest and see if anything more can be squeezed out of their tough hides. Your role will be to soften them up here and try to determine if they may know more than we are getting from them. Listening and trying to determine if what they say corresponds with any earlier sessions here will be an important part of what you do. We need to know if they are playing games with us. It might help to loosen some of them up if you just converse with them a bit. God knows what some of these blokes have done since the war began, and we need to know as much as possible about their roles if we can get them talking."

Frieda listened intently and frowned, saying, "Well, if they are as fanatic as I've been told, it doesn't seem as though they will be too interested in giving us much except their names and some dirty looks."

Smythe replied, "We haven't had a woman here before, and so you could say this is an experiment our intelligence agencies want to try. These blokes are men and, of course, good-looking women are of some interest to them, so don't underestimate the power of your good looks. A friendly demeanor can sometimes do wonders in obtaining cooperation and, in this case, information."

And so began Frieda's stay at Camp Woodhouselee. Her day of work usually began around 10:00 in the morning. She would walk from her rooms or breakfast to a special office set up outside of the main camp. Her first activity would be to discuss the day's interrogations with the intelligence interrogator from London and then review any of the previous files that have been accumulated for prisoners. She and the interrogator would decide which of the prisoners would be subject to meeting her first.

Shortly after, the first of the prisoners would be brought into the room by the military police. For those who were to be softened up, Frieda would greet them in her Bavarian-flavored German and begin asking about their families and if they thought they were safe from the bombings. If they were willing to converse, she would continue in a friendly mode, discussing what might be happening in the area where the prisoner's family lived and how they might be faring. She would offer them the chance to write to their families using special prisoner of war forms provided by the Red Cross. Some of the prisoners would begin to discuss the war and their homes; others would not pick up a discussion or would just tell her to forget it, that they knew what she was trying to do and then refuse to say more.

～

Time passed and Frieda stayed on the job until mid-August, 1943, interviewing the German personnel in the camp. Her reports and viewpoints on German military and civilian conditions were numerous, along with other information she thought might interest the British Intelligence Services. Unbeknownst to her, she was becoming very well thought of by those in charge and they were conveying their appreciation of Frieda's efforts to the OSS back in Washington.

One cloudy, windy day, something happened to bring a ray of sunshine into Frieda's life in Scotland. She had just finished lunch and had gone back to the interrogation office. A military policeman escorted a German SS Scharführer into the office just after she sat down at her desk. Frieda directed him to sit down, smiled, introduced herself, and in her friendliest voice, asked him his name and rank and where he served.

"My name is Franz Mueller. Rank is Scharführer," he replied.

"How long have you been in the SS, Herr Mueller?" Frieda asked.

"Much too long, Fraulein. I'm from Karlsfeld, near Munich, and my family is there. I'm afraid that they are going to be in the bombing. I've been here in this camp now for a month. I've had no word from them since several months before I was captured. Are you able to help me find out if they are still alive and well?"

"I can certainly try," she said and then discussed the Red Cross prisoner of war forms. "You will need to send one of the forms home on a regular basis. They are sent to Germany through a mail transfer office in Lisbon. Your family will need to know that you are well and where to send mail to you."

Frieda's curiosity rose when she heard Mueller was from the Munich area. "So you lived near Munich, Herr Mueller. I lived there for a number of years and went to the university. I thought the city and its suburban areas were very historic and interesting and I attended many events in and around the city. Did you have employment there before the war?"

Frieda's answer disarmed Mueller who, while he was in the SS, was certainly from a different mold than some of the other SS personnel at the camp. "I was a traffic policeman for a number of years before the war broke out. When that happened, everything changed. Fairly soon, demands for men for combat duty started to come and had priority over directing traffic. I found myself stuffed into an SS uniform and sent to Dachau Concentration Camp to assist in controlling the camp."

Frieda was jolted when she heard the word Dachau, but she kept her emotions in check and hoped Mueller didn't notice. "Herr Mueller, if they needed combat troops why did they send you to the camp? That was far from the front lines and certainly much safer."

Mueller snorted and said, "Things at the camp could be as bad as combat, Fraulein. It was not a pleasant duty station, although my job was not as bad as some. I was a driver assisting the SS Arbeitseinsatzführer who was looking after the work assignments of men in the camp. I drove him around and then, when needed, acted as a guard and driver for moving prisoners around between the main camp and their work stations."

Frieda became mildly excited hearing this and practically blurted out, "I knew someone who was sent to Dachau from the university and my last information about him was that he was working in a paper factory in the village. Maybe you have driven him there but that, of course, would be a coincidence given the many people in the camp."

Mueller looked at her for a moment and said, "Yes, it would be a coincidence, but as a matter of fact I did drive someone they called the Professor at different times. I'm not sure of his name, but I don't think he was a German. I was driving workers from the section of the camp that housed political and criminal prisoners."

Frieda held her breath but managed to say, "Do you remember what he looked like? He might have been my professor at the university. He disappeared one day. No one seemed to know what happened to him. A year or so ago someone who had lived in Germany and still had some way to contact people there told me he was in Dachau."

Mueller thought for a moment before he answered, "He was a tall man and quite good looking. One of the last places I took him was to the porcelain works in Allach. I believe he was given a job there of some sort, and I took him to the prisoner compound where he was to be housed while he worked in the factory. The prisoners in those special work places were not treated as roughly as were some of the other prisoners. And those lucky enough to work at Allach were treated especially good as the factory was a hobby for Reichsführer Himmler. The Allach Director was careful that the people working were presentable and not in a physical condition where they would make mistakes. They were producing the best porcelain in Germany. As far as I know, he was still there when I got transferred out of Dachau."

Frieda was almost overwhelmed with emotion at that point and somehow she knew in her heart that she had just received news of her Dirk. Even though the Scharführer's memory was not complete, he had said enough to convince Frieda that Dirk was alive and well. Her elation was so great that she could hardly finish the interrogation and the others the rest of the day. She thought to herself that if she could, she would ask the London interrogation specialist if she could call Mueller back and try and pry more information out of him if it was possible.

But this was not to be. The next morning she was sitting with several of the other women at breakfast when Captain Smythe walked into the dining hall and came directly to her. "Frieda, when you have finished your breakfast, please report to me in my office."

Frieda went shortly after to Smythe's office and sat down near his desk while he finished signing some papers that were spread out in front of him. He looked up and smiled, saying, "Good morning, Frieda. I have some interesting news for you from London. I'm not sure how much you know of the American OSS and what they have been doing lately, but they have not lost track of the fact that you have been on loan to us. I received a call from our London headquarters late yesterday. They are asking for you to be brought off loan to us and return to work for their organization. So I am arranging travel for you to return to London and be debriefed by our people and then released to the OSS."

Frieda was immediately disappointed that her efforts to question Scharführer Mueller were going to be interrupted. She didn't show any emotion, though, and Captain Smythe continued. "Please use the rest of the day to close out your affairs here, and later this afternoon please come back to our office and pick up your tickets for London. Sergeant Craig will have them at the reception desk.

"Frieda, you've been a real asset for us here and your efforts have helped us to put together some very important intelligence on the enemy. I'm very grateful for what you have done and the way you've done it and we have made that known to our London people and the OSS. I'm writing up a summary of your work and its success to put in your file. My best wishes to you for your future work. I think that the success of your work with us has convinced the OSS people that they can use your talents in other ways." Smythe got up and came over to Frieda and shook her hand. "I really hate to see you leave, but I know that duty calls and you will make good use of your skills at your next assignment. This is all about defeating Germany and that is what all of us have to keep in mind."

Frieda returned to London and reported to British Intelligence headquarters. She was given several days off and was told to report to the Unit Commanding Officer, Major McConnell, which she did the following Monday. "Ms. de Vries, I needn't tell you the value you have been to us and our service. Captain Smythe has already done that and all I can add is that we will always be grateful for the way you have conducted yourself and the sterling service you have given Great Britain. I'd like to give you this commendation, signed by the Commander of all British Intelligence Services, as a way of showing how important you have been to us. There are not many agents who receive this in our units here in Britain, and I am pleased to say that you're one of them. Good luck on your reassignment back to the OSS."

The next day, Frieda took a cab through the bomb-scarred streets of London to the Mayfair section of the city where the OSS offices were located at 72 Grosvenor Street. Many secret missions were planned and sent on their way from this office during the final days of the war. Frieda entered the building and was escorted to an office where she would be interviewed and perhaps given her new assignment. Shortly after sitting down in the empty office, a tall man dressed in civilian clothes entered and said, "Frieda, I'm David Bruce. We're glad to have you back with our organization. How was your stay with British Intelligence? I understand they were very pleased at what you did for them in interrogating prisoners and gathering and reporting on information you and others had collected."

Frieda, still disappointed at not being able to find out more about Dirk from the SS man in Scotland, said, "Well, it was very interesting work on a professional and personal basis. I would have liked to stay a bit longer, but I understand the urgency of what all these intelligence-gathering efforts have for the conduct of the war."

Bruce chatted with her for a while in order to get a better picture of all she had been doing at the Scottish prisoner-of-war camp. As their discussion wound down, Frieda told him, "So you can see that I am ready for another assignment and a change of scenery."

David Bruce smiled and said, "I'm glad to hear that. You're going to have a change of scenery in a big way if you accept this assignment. We would like you to work for us in Switzerland — Bern, to be exact. That will be a little different from where you were at Milton Bridge in the boondocks of Scotland. A man by the name of Allen Dulles is running the show in Bern and is interested in you because of your ability to speak German like a native. For the record, you will be assigned to the offices at the American Embassy and will work for them as a translator whenever Dulles has no immediate assignment for you. He will be your immediate OSS supervisor and will determine your assignments and where he might want you to work."

The thought of going to Switzerland to work gave Frieda a momentary thrill. She would be surrounded by the Axis forces — in France, Italy, Germany, and Austria — and would be once again within a few hundred kilometers of Dachau and the man with whom she had fallen in love and bonded. The thrill was only momentary, however, as her thoughts abruptly turned to her assignment and what it might bring. Would she be up to it? Would it be dangerous? She looked at Bruce and said, "I'm ready to go and I look forward to working with Allen Dulles. My work so far has been more or less crunching intelligence for the OSS and the British. I'm not sure what kind of work Dulles might want me to do, but I certainly know all about conditions in Europe and what the war is doing to people there — both our friends and foes. I can't say that I'm going into this blind. When will I leave and how will I get there?"

Bruce shuffled through some papers before he answered, "It appears that Dulles will be going to Bern in November. I think it would be wise for you to travel there sometime soon so you can be settled and ready for whatever it is that you will have to do. I'll have our people arrange for you to fly to Lisbon where you will meet an agent who will accompany you across the border into France and then into Switzerland. So far, we are able to get into Switzerland through the unoccupied portion of France. So, please be ready to travel on Sunday next."

Frieda had almost a week in which she explored London and visited the many historical points of interest that are in the city. But her interest in them was muted as she saw the damage that the German air raids had caused. Several times the sirens sounded, warning the populace of an air attack, and she, along with a host of glum faced Londoners, traipsed down into the air raid shelters to escape possible death.

During the week, a messenger brought Frieda instructions for the trip. She must report to the OSS headquarters at 0600 hours, and she would be escorted from there to the airfield from whence she would fly. When Sunday came, Frieda was ready, and, just before 0600, an American Ford staff car drove up by her building, picked her up, and departed for the airport. Frieda was tense. While she had experienced danger during her days in Germany and the leafleting campaign, it was before the general war had broken out and any danger then came from being arrested by the Gestapo instead of being shot down now while flying in a war zone. Nevertheless, she boarded the DC-3 at the Great West military airport at Heathrow, used by the OSS, and it took off for a secret military airport at Winkleigh, Devon.

An hour later, Frieda looked down at the rural Devon countryside as the flight circled the airfield before landing. The area was mostly farmland and its sunny green pastures and hedges belied the intense activity taking place at the airfield. Winkleigh Airfield was used by the U.S. Air Force, as well as the British, Canadian, and Polish, and was a major point for the transporting of Allied personnel, spies, or resistance agents to and from occupied Europe. However, along with its other uses, it was used as a point of departure for diplomatic personnel heading for Portugal, Spain, and Switzerland. Frieda's stay at Winkleigh was short.

As she waited in a terminal-like office building, the afternoon waned into early evening, and she was escorted to another DC-3 that took off for Lisbon, Portugal, within moments of her settling down. Several other persons were passengers on the flight, but they were obviously not English or American and did not seem communicative. The flight flew well to the west of France in growing darkness to avoid any intercepting German fighter aircraft and touched down at the Lisbon Airfield four hours later. As the DC-3 rolled to a stop, Frieda felt an uncontrollable welling up of emotion and broke into tears to the surprise of her fellow passengers. She was at last on the same continent as her lost Dirk and her heart filled with despair and sadness thinking of him and where he might be. And yet, the touchdown gave her hope again that she would be able to find out something about whether or not he was still among the living.

DC-3 (Courtesy of Towpilot via GNU Free Documentation License)

Into the Soviet Union's Endless Steppes

The staff car that Hauptsturmführer Radtke had requisitioned from the SD unit in Lvov rattled along on the rutted dirt road through the countryside east of the city. Behind it, a small canvas covered truck followed, driven by a SS-Mann assigned to the Lvov police unit. The truck carried a number of large barrels and tools to be used for digging and shoveling. Dirk sat in the rear seat of the staff car between two of the Dachau guards. Both men had their machine pistols on their laps. Radtke was in the front passenger seat while the third Dachau guard drove the vehicle.

The small convoy was headed for a clay site that had been mined by several Ukrainian porcelain producers prior to the German occupation. This was the site that had interested Obersturmbannführer Diebitsch. Radtke intended to look the site over, make an initial determination on the quality of the clay, and, if warranted, collect a good sample supply and return to the Allach factory. After testing, if the clay was as good as it had been rumored, Diebitsch would work out an arrangement for obtaining a steady supply.

The countryside through which they traveled was partly forested and partly open and slightly rolling. It was a warm spring day, and as they traveled through a coppice of spruce and pine trees, the car driver suddenly uttered an oath and pulled off to the side of the road with a jolt. "Ach, sir, I saw metal flashing in the woods to the right. We may be driving into a trap," he told Radtke. The two guards by Dirk clutched their machine pistols and rolled out on either side of the car just as several bullets banged into the vehicle and flattened one of the tires.

Radtke yelled, "Get this turned around," as he jumped out and ran back toward the following truck. As he approached the truck, several bursts of automatic weapon fire crashed into it, one of which went through the windshield and killed the driver. Dirk crouched down in the back seat of the car on the floor. Several more bullets ricocheted off the side of the car as the two Dachau guards fired their weapons into the woods. Both men had taken cover in a ditch beside the road.

Radtke shouted at all of them, "Forget the car, let's get this truck turned around and get out of here." Dirk didn't budge. The car was disabled and partially in the ditch and was useless as an escape vehicle. The guards scurried in the ditch back to the truck. Meanwhile, Radtke had yanked the dead driver out of the vehicle and proceeded to turn it around on the narrow road. The Dachau guards kept firing their machine pistols into the woods on both sides of the road, and it seemed to suppress any concentrated fire at the truck. The guards jumped into the back of the truck and Radtke tramped on the gas and they gathered speed. The guards kept firing as they bumped down the road.

Dirk was a sacrifice as far as they were concerned and they had no intention of going back for him. Radtke yelled to one of the guards through the back window in the truck cab, "If they leave him alive, we'll get him when we go back there." He picked up the truck radio and called in to Lvov and told the police dispatcher there what had happened.

"We'll have a patrol out there within an hour. Get out of the general area and pick a place where the unit can meet you," he told Radtke.

The forest was quiet after the truck left the scene and Dirk remained crouched in the back seat of the staff car. He heard the grinding of the truck engine getting fainter as it put distance between it and the ambush. After a short time, he heard several voices and boots crunching on the dirt road, and as he peeked out, several men in civilian clothes came out of the woods and examined the dead SS man, kicked him several times, and collected his weapons and emptied his pockets.

Then they looked at the staff car and walked down the road toward it. Other men were now visible standing in the woods and several of them also approached the car. Dirk ducked his head and stayed where he was. One of the men walked up to the side of the car and peered in and said in Russian, "Ah, we have one of the devils here in the car." He pulled open the door and shoved a pistol into Dirk's back. "Out, with your hands up," he yelled. Dirk raised his hands and backed out of the car. Someone hit him in the back with the butt of a rifle. "Turn around, you Nazi pig," one of them yelled in broken German. Dirk slowly turned around expecting at any moment to be shot down by the group of men now surrounding him. He didn't say a word.

"Why are you out of uniform? Who are you and what are you doing here?" the man screamed.

A tall man with a leather cap walked up as Dirk was about to answer and said in Russian, "Kavitsky, I'll handle this." In almost flawless German, he said to Dirk, "Answer the questions."

Dirk, swallowed hard and said in as even a voice as he could, "I'm from the Dachau Konzentrationlager near Munich in Germany. I was brought here to help the people you chased away. I was to do some of the heavy work for them." Dirk showed them his Dachau prisoner tattoo and pointing into the vehicle, he continued, "My jacket in the car, you will notice, has a red triangle sewn onto it. I was a political prisoner and have been in the forced-labor program at Dachau since I was picked up by the Gestapo in 1940." Dirk noticed a red star on the cap of the man now interrogating him. He reasoned he was evidently confronted by a group of partisans operating behind the German front line.

"That doesn't explain what you are doing here. Why were these dogs out here and what devilment were you up to?" the tall man snorted.

Dirk explained what they were doing in the Ukraine to the obviously incredulous interrogator. The man listened until Dirk had finished and then yelled to his group, "Set this vehicle on fire and let's get out of here. You can be sure that they will be back here with a mob of the Feldgendarmerie to try and round us up. There will be too many of them to stay and fight. As for you," he said to Dirk, "welcome to the Ukrainian Soviet Socialist Republic.

"If your story holds water and we decide you aren't fabricating it, you can consider yourself to have been liberated. We'll be happy to draft you into our group as a volunteer. You can become a fighter with us for the defeat of the Germans. I'm sure that you will enjoy taking part in the coming battles, having had to endure captivity for so long. Now, let's get out of here before the place is swarming with the SS. You can be sure that we will do some further questioning about this absurd mission your buddies and you were on. I am Commissar Vokoi, by the way."

At this moment, Dirk's heart couldn't have dropped any lower. *I have gone from the frying pan, not into the fire, but into the furnace*, he thought to himself. As the small, armed group marched away through the trees and brush, Dirk wondered if he would ever see Frieda and Holland again. He had no idea that the war would grind on for almost another two years with the deaths of millions of additional victims.

Identifies Field Police or Gendarmes. German military police units wore duty gorgets around their necks on chains on their upper chests, thus they obtained the nickname of "chain dogs".

The war would be a testimony to one more nation, this time Germany, led astray by the promises of an ideology and a nation's leaders who hid their agendas and intentions and were freely elected to power by a duped public. It seems that history repeats itself again and again as new generations come on to the scene and refuse to learn from the lessons of the past.

Frieda Moves to Switzerland

Frieda was met at the Lisbon airport by a young man who introduced himself as Paul. "Hello, Frieda. I've been sent to see that you get to a hotel tonight and then get off in the morning on time. We've got a hotel set up for you nearby and you should be comfortable and able to get a good night's rest."

He picked up Frieda's luggage and went to a waiting automobile and without much conversation drove to the hotel. Frieda was picked up again early in the morning and driven back to the airport. By 0800 she was onboard a Spanish passenger aircraft bound for Madrid and Barcelona. She arrived in Barcelona in the afternoon and once again had to stay overnight at a hotel.

The morning dawned bright and cloudless as her Swiss Air flight took off on time and headed toward Bern. As they flew, they were over the azure glistening Mediterranean Sea for some time, and then as they turned and headed northeast, it slowly faded away behind them. Soon they were over the jagged peaks of the Alps. Frieda looked down on the craggy scene below and wondered what lay ahead. She wasn't aware when the aircraft crossed the Spanish frontier and was in Swiss air space until it slowly began to descend. The plane finally landed at the Bern airfield without any difficulties. As soon as she entered the terminal, she was approached by a young woman who appeared to be somewhat older than she.

"Hello there, you must be Frieda. We've been expecting you. How was your trip?" she said as she approached Frieda and reached out to shake her hand.

"The trip was somewhat frightening and I'm glad to be

here, without a doubt. I haven't flown anywhere before where enemy aircraft may shoot you down and it wasn't something that I enjoyed," Frieda said.

The young woman responded by introducing herself. "I'm Stephanie Chew and I'll be working with you at the embassy. They've sent me down to meet you and make sure that you arrived safe and sound and to get you set up in your new home."

They gathered Frieda's luggage and were soon on their way into the city. As they drove along, Frieda told Stephanie a little about herself and where she was from and was surprised to learn that Stephanie was from the other end of Pennsylvania in a suburb of Pittsburgh. Somehow, knowing someone from back home gave her a feeling of comfort.

They chatted about home, parents, and the war and what it was doing to Europe. Even Switzerland in its neutrality had not avoided trouble as both Allied and German planes had bombed some of the Swiss towns near the German border. The Swiss were continually complaining to both belligerent sides about intrusions into their air space and had warned each that they were ready to shoot intruders down if it didn't stop.

Frieda and Stephanie soon arrived at the Bellevue Palace Hotel on Kochergasse and Frieda's luggage was snapped up by an attendant and taken into the building. "You've lucked out, Frieda," said Stephanie. "This will be your new home. They've arranged for you to have a small suite where you can cook and be at home if you don't want to eat out. Swiss food is pretty scrumptious, though. By the way, the language in this part of Switzerland is German."

"Yes, I know. I had a nice briefing in London before coming here and it was a relief to know I wouldn't have to learn Italian or French while I work here," Frieda said.

Stephanie went up to Frieda's room and stayed for a while and talked. She set up a weekend date with Frieda so that she could show her around and help get her oriented. She also mentioned that Frieda would be picked up the following Monday to meet her supervisor at the embassy and begin work. Frieda was tense and tired after her journey from London and a respite of a few days before having to work sounded very good to her. It would also give her a chance to familiarize herself with the city that was to be her home until the end of the war.

Monday came all too fast. Stephanie picked Frieda up early in the morning and took her to the American Embassy. Mr. Harrison, the ambassador, was out in one of the Swiss Cantons so Stephanie took her in to introduce her to the ambassador's first secretary.

"I'm very pleased to meet you Ms. de Vries. I've been aware that you were on your way here to assist Mr. Dulles when he arrives. I hope your trip wasn't too uncomfortable. Given the war, there are very few options left to get people from the States or Britain here."

"Are the arrangements made for your living quarters to your liking?" John Phillips, the first secretary, asked with a smile. Frieda, who very much liked the Bellevue Plaza, replied, "Oh, they couldn't be better. I have everything I need and more. I also found that there are quite a few people from all over the world staying off and on at the hotel. I'm sure that this may be a plus when I'm doing some of Mr. Dulles' work. So, I'm anxious to begin. I know Mr. Dulles won't be here until November, but I'm sure that I can make myself useful to the embassy until then."

Phillips nodded in agreement. "We can certainly find some work for you here, as there's a constant flow of émigrés from the various occupied countries and Germany, and we need someone who can converse with them. Plus, we have made room for a certain number of our Jewish friends from the occupied countries who somehow managed to get across the Swiss border. I'm sure that being in touch with such a varied cross-section of people will give you some inspiration and perhaps a preview of what to expect when Mr. Dulles gets here."

Phillips then took Frieda on a tour of the Embassy building and introduced her to most of the staff. Frieda had her own office on the top floor of the building. Stephanie's office was adjacent to hers. It turned out that she, too, was to work for Allen Dulles, the new station chief for the OSS operations in Switzerland. And so a month passed and November was upon Frieda, who hardly noticed the passage of the days. Her ability with the German language brought her a continual stream of opportunities to act as an interpreter with a variety of characters who were of interest to the embassy or came to it for some type of help. She did this for the various embassy departments. From what she learned, she wrote reports on what these people revealed about their circumstance and their experiences outside of Switzerland. Her work became even more interesting than it had been interrogating German prisoners of war.

Mr. Dulles finally arrived by rail from the border of the unoccupied portion of France in early November. Soon after he crossed it, German troops occupied the southern portion of France and the border was closed. Following that, there were no other ways to get in or out of Switzerland except by some circuitous or surreptitious and very dangerous means.

Dulles' arrival did little to change Frieda's current work routines for the time being. He made it a point to visit the embassy as soon as he arrived and meet the ambassador and first secretary. Following that, he was brought to Frieda's office to meet her. He entered the room and immediately extended his hand and stridently said, "I am so glad to meet you. I've followed your work for some time now and have been impressed with what you've done. You seem to have a knack in turning out well-thought-out and accurate reports from the raw facts you've gathered. I know that we'll be able to work together very well for as long as this war lasts."

Frieda thanked him for his kind words and said, "Well, I hope that I can continue in that vein. It's been an interesting three or four years for me working for the OSS in Washington and helping British Intelligence. I also had an acute learning experience as a student at the university in Munich before departing Germany with the Gestapo on my heels."

Dulles laughed and said, "Yes, we had some up-to-the-minute information about your experiences there from your old friend Hans who lived near your uncle and aunt. You probably didn't know we were on to you way back when, did you?"

Frieda laughed. "Well, to me at the time, it was no laughing matter and I was too focused on what we were doing to even consider that anyone in the United States would even care what we were doing. A lot of my energy was derived from the knowledge that a very close friend of mine was in the concentration camp at Dachau."

"Ah, yes," Dulles said as he nodded and lit up his pipe. "Hans told me about that. Perhaps in the coming months we might be able to find out something about your friend. We'll have to see how things develop here. Now, I've got a lot to do to get things set up as well as find some place to live. You won't hear from me for a while but be ready, we'll be getting busy one of these days soon."

With that, he left the room and went to Stephanie's office to meet her. Frieda was impressed with Dulles' booming laugh and what seemed to her to be a good sense of humor. He appeared to be a man with strong drive and much energy for whatever he would decide to do. She thought that the future ought to be quite an interesting time. His reference to the Spider and, of course, the fact that he had mentioned trying to trace the whereabouts of Dirk, stirred in her a feeling that she would do all she could to help this man in his work.

Dulles busied himself for the rest of the year in finding a place to live and beginning to make contacts he would need to gather information that would help defeat the Germans. He moved into a rented apartment on the ground floor of a large villa at Herrengasse 23 in the older part of the city. His presence as an assistant to the American ambassador was announced in the press. A Geneva newspaper told the world that he was a representative of President Roosevelt and would be carrying out special duties. Dulles and the OSS were happy about the publicity, as it would increase his chances of positive interactions with the various personages and groups congregating in this neutral country.

Dulles came from a well-to-do family of lawyers and had graduated with a Masters Degree from Princeton University. He entered the Foreign Service in 1916 and worked in various Foreign Service positions including one in Bern during World War I, when he became involved in gathering intelligence. Later, he wanted a change and went back to school to earn a law degree. He took a position with his brother at a prestigious law firm in New York that had offices and contacts all over the world.

When the OSS was created, "Wild Bill" Donavan, its director who knew Dulles, asked him to work for the organization again in the Bern office. Since Bern was surrounded by Axis or Axis-occupied nations, it was a virtual hotbed of intrigue. Foreign diplomats, spies, secret agents, travelers, refugees, international businessmen, German laborers, Catholic and Protestant clergymen, and various anti-Nazi German exiles were crawling up the walls.

Herrengasse 23 (Courtesy of Sandstein via Creative Commons License)

Dulles came to the job with a desire to defeat the Nazi presence in Europe, but he also wanted to lay the groundwork for developing information about the Soviet Union. His positions with the Foreign Service and his law firm had firmly entrenched him in American society's capitalist upper classes. He was an advocate of its views of international engagement where America would be the dominating force. This upper crust of wealthy people manipulated the business world, the government, and the nation's population; Dulles was one who would use his position in government to perpetuate and further his and their aims.

His actions during the close of World War II transitioned quickly from battling the Nazis to opposing socialism and communism in Europe. He would play a major role in the war the Western nations, led by the U.S., later conducted against the Soviet Union. The trumpet call to the American and other Western nation's populations was that we were now in The Cold War and should arm ourselves in order to resist and undermine any successes of the Soviet Union's socialist and communist system.

Dulles began making contacts with many individuals and groups as soon as he had his personal concerns settled. Frieda was put to work and the work turned out to be more varied and interesting than she ever imagined. She became heavily involved in the many parties, teas, dinners, and meetings that Dulles held at the Legation, his apartment, and in other locations in Bern and other parts of Switzerland. Frieda's youth, good looks, friendliness, and ability to speak both English and German helped to make her a welcome and popular addition to the events Dulles created.

Frieda was given the job of developing profiles on as many of these people as Dulles thought necessary and was tasked to set up a filing system so that the profiles were available as needed. She found herself on call at times when she thought she was really on her own time. She traveled with Dulles to the various Swiss locations he visited and kept a log of these travels, why they traveled, and with whom they visited or had contacts. She had to code and decode messages that Dulles was sending or receiving from OSS headquarters as well as to and from the many agents that were in the field.

Her knowledge of the affairs of this Bern spymaster grew as the time passed. And the time did pass—faster now that she was heavily involved in her work. The months of 1943 and early 1944 seemed to disappear as soon as the calendar page was turned. Frieda concentrated hard on her work. She had all the social life she needed in the whirlwind of events in which Dulles was constantly involved. Occasionally, she would accept a request for a date from someone she met at a party or elsewhere.

She never took her mind off her lost partner, however, keeping her current relationships as simple as possible. If someone appeared to be moving toward a more serious and intimate relationship, she would cut it off. Although the months were passing, the disappointment of losing Dirk still overwhelmed her when she thought of him in the quiet of her apartment or when she was out in the city parks or the surrounding countryside. The war continued to go on around this Swiss island of neutrality. It more and more was unfavorable to the Nazi regime and setbacks continued to bleed the Reich of its men and resources.

Sometime in April of 1944, she was in her office in the legation when she received a surprise telephone call. She picked up the phone and greeted the caller. The voice on the other end of the line was that of the Spider. "Frieda, it's good to hear your voice. I hope that all goes well with you," he said. Frieda had not forgotten about Spider but her work kept her so busy that she seldom thought about him or the role he played earlier in her life.

"Hans, I can't believe it's you. Are you well and where are you?" Frieda blurted out.

"I'm okay. I'm a little older and worse for the wear but still around. I'm in Switzerland for a short time and would like to meet with you sometime soon. I have some information that might be of interest to you," he said. "I'd just as soon stay away from the embassy, if you don't mind." Frieda didn't question this, as she knew that Hans wanted to remain as anonymous as possible for his own self-protection. She asked him when he would like to meet and said that she was available anytime in the near future. They agreed on a small café near the Legation and a week later Frieda and Spider once again faced each other.

Spider was already occupying a table in the café when Frieda walked in. He stood up when he saw her and they embraced almost without thinking as Frieda came close. "You look healthy and happy, Frieda, and I must say I'm glad to see you again after so many months," he exclaimed.

"Hans, I've thought about you over the past months and wondered if you were okay and what you were doing," she answered as they sat down and ordered tea.

"Well, I've kept pretty busy, especially when I've been in German territory and trying to dodge the bombs and bullets. But as you can see, I'm still all in one piece. But the reason I'm here today is that I've brought you news from deep inside the Third Reich," he announced somewhat triumphantly, as he knew how much Frieda wanted information about Dirk.

Frieda gulped, almost choking on a sip of tea. "I hope it's

something I want to hear," she exclaimed. "I've had all the bad news I can stand in one lifetime. What's the news?"

Spider looked at her with a smile and said, "I've found someone who knew some things about Dirk. But I don't want you to get your hopes up, though. He is a German carpenter who was doing some work for the SS at the Allach Porcelain Factory. He actually worked with Dirk on something or other in the factory. He knew Dirk's name and told me it was de Vries."

Frieda felt somewhat faint at hearing this but managed to stay calm. "What did he say, Hans?" she whispered.

"Well, he said that he had met Dirk when they worked together for several weeks inside the factory. From what he could tell, Dirk appeared to be healthy. He said he did not seem to be starving to death like some of the people in the Dachau Camp that he had seen. He was able to do carpentry work without any trouble. He told my carpenter that he was going to be leaving on a trip shortly and didn't know when he would be back. He indicated that it was to somewhere in the Soviet Union. My carpenter got the impression that Dirk wasn't being transferred to another camp, but he was going there with some of the factory administrators and would be back to the factory after the trip was over. The carpentry project ended shortly after that so he was uncertain if and when Dirk ever left for the trip or got back to the factory," Spider told her.

Frieda could not believe that she was hearing such good news. "Hans, this is the best news I've heard since I left Washington. I just knew that if I came back to Europe I might somehow find out more about what has happened to Dirk. When did you find out this news?" she asked, to confirm that he still could be alive even while they sat in the café. Spider told her it was sometime in 1943. Frieda was a little disappointed that so many months had passed before she found this out. "I'm glad you took the trouble to come here and tell me this, Hans. Thanks."

They chatted and reminisced for some time about their contacts over the years. Spider knew better than to query Frieda about what she was doing and that if he did she would only tell him she was a clerk at the Legation. And Frieda knew not to question Spider. They embraced in the late afternoon and Spider said, as he was getting ready to leave, "It's a relief knowing that you're doing so well, and I'm glad I took a little side trip here to make you feel a little better. I'll continue to be watchful about Dirk and if I can find out more, I'll let you know about it. It's getting tougher and tougher to get into the Reich now, and it may be impossible one of these days. I've got to go now, so I'll say goodbye, Frieda. Keep well." Spider left the café and almost immediately was lost in the crowded street.

Again, the months passed. The war continued and thousands died every day in a grim testimonial to the glory of the war. A large German army was defeated at the battle for Stalingrad in the Soviet Union. From then on, the German, Italian, Romanian, and Hungarian armies were pushed back as the Red Army began its deadly march from the east to Berlin. Meanwhile, British, American, Canadian, and free French and Polish troops participated in the invasion of France on the European western front.

A conspiracy in 1944 occurred among German Wehrmacht officers who attempted to assassinate Hitler but failed. And nothing changed. The situation for Hitler and the German people became even more desperate as the year came to a close. Frieda continued her work with Allen Dulles and the OSS, and it seemed that there was never a dull moment. She watched and waited for the Spider to reappear and bring her the news that Dirk was alive and well and ready to rejoin her, but it never came. While she was distracted by work, she didn't have time to think much about Dirk's situation. But when she was alone, her mind began to dwell more and more on him as she knew that very soon the war would be over and people could once again pick up what was left of their lives. Would Dirk be in her arms once again?

During the last year of the war, members of the German Wehrmacht and the SS began to seriously question their duty to their Führer and how far it should be carried. The armed services of Germany had committed themselves by oath to serve their Führer and obey his orders. But the reality of Germany's situation appeared to be hopeless and the war could not end any other way than by the nation's defeat. The war had consumed hundreds of thousands of German men in their prime along with thousands of other combatant soldiers and millions of civilians.

So it was with SS-Obergruppenführer Karl Wolff, commander of all SS and police formations in occupied Italy. As the invading force of American and British forces fought their way north, toward the portion of Italy ruled by the dictator Mussolini but actually controlled by the SS and police, Wolff decided to attempt to stop the bloodshed in Italy independently and without the approval of SS-Reichsführer Himmler or his Führer Adolph Hitler. Wolff had long been associated as an advisor to Himmler and a liaison between Himmler and Hitler, and, as such, he had access to the two most powerful men in the Third Reich.

As he began efforts to contact President Roosevelt's representative, Allen Dulles, in Bern, Switzerland, he was unaware that his efforts coincided with those of two other powerful men in the SS. Reichsführer. Himmler was trying to do the same through contacts in Sweden and SS-Obergruppenführer. Ernst Kaltenbrunner, Chief of the Reich Security Main Office, was attempting to negotiate with the Allied powers through Dulles.

Wolff began his efforts to contact Western powers and stop the fighting in Italy through an intermediary, Baron Luigi Parilla, in February 1945. Parilla made contact with a friend in Switzerland, Dr. Max Husmann, to begin the effort. Husmann knew a Swiss army officer and member of the Swiss Secret Service, Max Waibal, who had contacts with Dulles. From that point on, there was much discussion about the sincerity of the SS in ending the bloodshed in Italy and to determine what the terms of any agreement might be.

Frieda played a role in some of the meetings, as Dulles had assigned her the duties of going with the negotiators to bring him an independent assessment of what actually took place. In early March, she attended a meeting in Lugano of Dulles' official representative, Paul Blum, with three intermediaries from Italy, Baron Parilla and two SS men, Standartenführer Eugen Dollmann, and Obersturmbannführer Guido Zimmer. Several other attendees came with the party from Italy, probably, Frieda thought, to act as witnesses.

Frieda and the witnesses sat near each other in the meeting room, and before the meeting began, they introduced themselves to each other. Frieda was unaware that one of the men, a young Hauptsturmführer by the name of Radtke, was the very same Radtke who had been with Dirk months before on the ill-fated trip to the Ukraine Soviet Socialist Republic. Because the meeting was very short, there was not much time for chatting. The men left hurriedly and Frieda and Blum returned to Bern.

The next meeting that Frieda was assigned to attend came later in March and took place at Ascona on Lake Maggiore. This time the meeting included two Allied generals, British Major General Terence Airy and American Major General Lyman Lemnitzer, as well as the top SS commander from Italy, Obergruppenführer Wolff. Following the meeting, Frieda found her way to a nearby overlook on the lake and sat down to enjoy the beauty of the scene in front of her. The weather was cool, but the sun was out and warming enough that Frieda knew spring would soon come to this mountainous country.

She had taken careful notes at the meeting and was glad to get a short respite from the intense effort she made to catch all that had been said. The silence was broken after a while by the voice of a man who had quietly walked up behind her, "Hello, Fraulein. How have you been?" It was Hauptsturmführer Radtke, who had been slowly strolling along the walk.

Surprised, Frieda turned and realized that it was one of the Germans attending the meeting. "I'm well, thanks," she responded. "I thought all of you were leaving soon."

The German smiled and said, "Alas, yes, we are leaving in the morning to go back to the war. Hopefully, the end of it is now only days away for us here in Italy and all I can say is the sooner the better. You speak German like you're a native. Are you Swiss or American?" he asked.

"No, I'm American, but I've lived with my aunt and uncle in Germany and spent some years at the university in Munich. My parents spoke German in our home in the U.S. I guess my German is good enough that they wanted me to work for our embassy here in Switzerland," Frieda replied.

Radtke, a bit surprised, said, "What a coincidence. I lived and worked a number of years outside of Munich. It is a great city, but I'm afraid that it has pretty much been bombed out now. I had relatives there, but they were killed in one of the raids."

Frieda offered her condolences and said, "The war has been one of the most awful things to hear and know about. I can only feel sorry for all the people whose lives have been disrupted and who have lost their relatives."

Her interest picked up a bit when Radtke had mentioned working near Munich, so she continued, "I learned to know Munich quite well. What kind of work did you do there?"

"Well," he said, glancing at his watch, "I was in the SS and worked at a porcelain factory in Allach."

Frieda swallowed hard. How could this be? Once again it seemed that fate had brought her together with someone who might know Dirk and where he might be. Was it too good to be true? Her voice tightened as she responded, "I had a very close friend from the university who was sent to the Dachau Camp and ended up working in Dachau at a factory and then at the porcelain works in Allach."

Radtke was somewhat surprised and said, "The plant was closed by Reichsführer Himmler last December. All of us in the military were reassigned, I was sent to Italy, and now here I am talking to a lovely fraulein in Switzerland. What was your friend's name?"

"His name was Dirk de Vries, and he had been a professor at the university in Munich." Frieda was now very tense as she sensed that she might at last know where Dirk was and what he would be doing. With the closure of the factory, she wondered if he was sent back to the main konzentrationlager.

Her response brought a gasp of surprise from Radtke and he stared hard at Frieda for an instant before he responded, "This is almost an unbelievable coincidence and meeting. I supervised Herr de Vries when I was at the factory. He was a good person and we got along well. He always seemed to want to learn about the jobs he was given and did well at them. He was an intelligent man but very quiet, probably because he wanted to stay at Allach — there were worse places to be.

"But I don't think you'll like what I'm going to tell you next." He then relayed to her the story of their expedition to the Ukraine and what had happened. "This was quite a while back, sometime in the spring or early summer of 1943. The Feldg-endarmerei from Lvov could find no trace of de Vries when they went to the ambush site. I'm so sorry I can't give you better news about him. The partisans may have captured him and killed him since he was with us or they may have drafted him to fight with them. In any event, he disappeared and we had no news of his whereabouts after that."

"Maybe the end of the war will allow him to return to you. Don't give up hope. Now, Fraulein, I must get back to our quarters before someone comes looking for me. Foreign military people are not very welcome in Switzerland. We are incognito and are closely supervised so there is no incident. It has been a pleasure speaking with you. I hope that efforts to end the fighting will succeed and, perhaps, we will see each other at another time and in happier circumstances." He reached out and shook her hand, bowed slightly, and then turned and started back the way he had come. Frieda, with tears clouding her eyes, watched his form recede as he made his way through the lengthening shadows of the afternoon toward the Villa in which the meeting had taken place.

The efforts of the OSS, the Allied Forces, and the SS in Italy ended the bloodshed there a week before Germany officially surrendered.

The Story Ends

Darkness was creeping over the city and filtering into the room as Adrian listened to the last of Mrs. de Vries' adventures as a member of the OSS. Mrs. de Vries had told her story and now appeared somewhat tired and dejected as she finished the tale. It was a sad tale and the ending was not a happy one that would please those who wish for happy endings. Neither one of them knew what had become of Dirk. As the war in Europe drew to a close, the final days of death, destruction, confusion, and sadness had hidden his fate as it had hidden the fate of millions of others. Whether he perished in the days that followed his "liberation" or whether he was still alive at the end of the war would remain a mystery. Europe was in chaos with thousands of refugees trying to find their way home.

The Allied nations had provoked Soviet Russia sufficiently during and at the end of the war that it severed most normal ties with the West. The break in ties resulted in the erection of what became known as the Iron Curtain. Whether Dirk still lived somewhere in the east behind this curtain would never be known. Western nations, fearful that communism might appeal to their people, began tilting the windmills of the so-called Cold War and normal communication and interchanges were mostly cut off by both sides.

When Mrs. de Vries had exhausted her story, Adrian sighed and looked out the window at the fading light. "It's almost unbelievable, Mrs. de Vries. All the things that happened to you and the troubles you've witnessed, as well as the loss of Dirk, are enough for two or three lifetimes. You never heard from Dirk again, I take it?" she asked, hoping that somehow, this frail woman in the last years of her life would reveal to her whether she and Dirk had formally exchanged wedding vows of holy matrimony. If indeed they had been married, civil records of birth, death, and marriage were very likely destroyed in the bombings.

She had spent many years living as Mrs. de Vries and somehow it must have meant something more than just a casual lover's relationship in the spring of their youth. Mrs. de Vies looked at Adrian and said, "No, never again did I hear from him, although I somehow knew he had survived the war. He was my lover, my companion, and my hero for those short wonderful years we were together. I proudly bear his name. My life was forever linked to his before his arrest. Anything else that might come to me could never be what he and I had together. Our souls and the Divine were united from the beginning, perhaps even before we were born.

"There are some relationships that one never can let go or terminate. Mine with him was one of them. Now, Adrian, you've heard the entire story. I'm tired and need to rest."

Adrian got up, gave Mrs. de Vries a hug, and let herself out through the front door.

GLOSSARY

Arbeitseinsatzführer: Labor Allocation Leader.

Aryan: A term referring to non-Jewish Caucasian persons with mostly Nordic type physical characteristics specified by Nazi racial experts as representing the pure Germanic master race.

Auschwitz: Concentration camp in Poland.

Autobahn: Super highway system constructed during Hitler's reign in Germany.

Babushka: A light cloth, usually square, placed over the head of a female with two loose ends tied under the chin.

CIA: Central Intelligence Agency. Gathers foreign intelligence for the U.S. Government and conducts secret operations to further foreign policy objectives.

Dachau: Village near Munich. Also location of a concentration camp where objectors to National Socialism were confined.

Fraulein: An unmarried lady.

Führer: Leader.

Gestapo: Abbreviation of the German words Geheime Staat Polizei, translating to Secret State Police.

Hauptmann: Rank of Captain in German Army.

Konzentrationlager: Concentration camp.

Leafleting: A propaganda and information tool used as an effective form of psychological warfare. It is used to try and alter the thinking and behavior of people and/or military troops in enemy territory. It was the main form of spreading messages to

152

a large number of people before the invention of technological electronic communication.

Levitation: Floating or hovering.

National Socialism: The name given to the political movement that brought Hitler to power.

Nazi: Abbreviation used in place of National Socialism.

OSS: Office of Strategic Service; Organization created to deal with the intelligence needs of the United States during the Second World War.

Quaker: Religious Christian group originating in England.

Sachsenhausen: Concentration camp northwest of Berlin.

SD: Initials standing for the German words Sicherheitdienst, translating to Security Service.

Sonderkommando: Selected concentration camp inmates who form a special squad mostly for the purpose of running the crematoria and other prisoner control duties. A metal identification disc indicated their special status.

SS: Initials standing for the German words Schutzstaffel, translating to Protection Guard.

Totenkopf: Deaths Head formation of the SS used mainly for the security and guarding of concentration camps. Later formed combat units as manpower needs grew in the war.

Wehrmacht: German armed forces.

Weimar Government: Government of Germany prior to the election of the Nazis to a majority in the Parliament.

SS Ranks and Equivalent U.S. Army Ranks

Reichsführer SS: Rank held only by Heinrich Himmler; Leader of SS in the Reich

Obergruppenführer: Army Commanding General

Standartenführer: Colonel

Hauptsturmbannführer: Colonel

Obersturmbannführer: Lieutenant Colonel

Sturmbannführer: Major

Hauptsturmführer: Captain

Obersturmführer: Lieutenant

Scharführer: Staff Sergeant

www.iwishyouweremine.com

www.ingramcontent.com/pod-product-compliance
Lightning Source LLC
Chambersburg PA
CBHW050736230626
47052CB00002BA/398

* 9 7 8 1 9 3 8 8 8 6 1 2 6 *